MISTAKE WISCONSIN

D1490551

Mistake, Wisconsin

Kersti Niebruegge

Kersti Niebruegge
New York

Copyright © 2014 by Kersti Niebruegge
All rights reserved. Published in the United States of America by Kersti Niebruegge, New York, NY.

Cover design and photograph by Kersti Niebruegge.
Photograph of author by Jayne Niebruegge.

ISBN (eBook): 978-0-9908710-0-2
ISBN (paperback): 978-0-9908710-1-9

Library of Congress Control Number: 2014920450

First Edition
December 2014

For all the kids who are forced to eat lutefisk.
Hang in there. There's gotta be meatballs somewhere.

ONE

Every cabin at Shady Pines Lodge proudly displayed tourism brochures from the newly formed chamber of commerce, just to make sure visitors knew of the amazing things the Northwoods could offer to folks not lucky enough to live there. Most guests tossed them right into the trash, but one of the new occupants of Cabin #8 Lil' Moose, Dan Schweitzman, read the earnest brochure while his two Chicago colleagues searched for a nonexistent Wi-Fi signal.

"The Mistake Chamber of Commerce welcomes you to Mistake, Wisconsin! We're really happy that you chose us for your vacation, because we realize how funny it is that the whole point of our founders naming the city Mistake was to discourage visitors," he read. "What can we say? Our great-great-grandparents wanted to keep the awesome musky fishing for themselves!

"Speaking of names and authenticity, we actually used to be called Swedetown. Technically, we could also be called New Zurich. Back in the nineteenth century, a Swiss explorer named Klaus Heffelfinger planted his flag in the cranberry bog at the center of town and declared the land

New Zurich in honor of his homeland. He probably regretted planting that flag because the bog instantly swallowed it—and him.

"A few years later, in the 1860s, dozens of immigrants from Sweden arrived at our town's borders. They had been following a trail of rune stones, those large raised stones with inscriptions from Vikings. The Swedes decided to set up shop and start farming, and thus began Swedetown!

"Subsequent archaeological research revealed that these iconic rune stones were, in fact, just run-of-the-mill rocks with hailstorm damage. The population grew, and our town was officially named Mistake in the late eighteen hundreds.

"As the largest city in Waumabenon County, Mistake is a community of 6,153 proud Mistakers on 151 square miles of land, 37 percent of which is water. We love our water activities! In the summer, you can enjoy fishing, tubing, and partying on a pontoon boat in one of our sixteen lakes. In the winter, you can ice skate on the lakes and then drill a hole and fish. If you're not into ice fishing, try driving your truck across the ice just because you can. It's pretty neat.

"If you happen to visit during the fall, have a tasty Friday fish fry at the Chitchat Supper Club, then spend your night enjoying prep football. We love our high school football team, the Mistake Muskies, which includes nearly every boy who attends our school. We're incredibly proud that football is a no-cut sport. Where else can you get that kind of community? We've won three—*three*—conference championships in the past eighty-four years!

"You might also want to try the world-famous lutefisk suppers served weekly at Mistake Lutheran Church (ELCA). That's right, *weekly* lutefisk suppers! While most towns in the Midwest only serve lutefisk during the holidays, you can get a big helping every Sunday evening in Mistake, unless it's during a Packers game. Check the church bulletin for replacement lutefisk lunch times.

"But let's get to the point, so you can start fishing! Whether you're joining us in the winter, summer, spring, or fall, there's plenty to do in Mistake, plenty of friendly people, and plenty of beer. Enjoy the fishing!"

Schweitzman closed the brochure. *Oh, we'll enjoy the fishing,* he thought. *And the beer.*

TWO

"That's OK, I've got it," Megan Svenson said to a three-year-old girl who had just knocked over a quart of dirt and earthworms. Megan had been playing with her phone, so she put it in her pocket and kneeled down. It was her thirty-ninth Saturday at the bait shop, so Megan was quite adept at chasing wiggling worms across the floor.

Tolerate was the best way to describe how fifteen-year-old Megan felt about working at Bart Brabender's bait shop, but she certainly wasn't going to quit and go work at her dad's custard stand with her fourteen-year-old sister, Lina. She'd been at Brabender's Bait for nearly a year and finally figured out that the best way to deal with the fish smell was to rub pumpkin pie spice on her neck, under her hair. It not only made her day smell better but also attracted guys who came into the bait shop, she thought.

It was verified and documented in her Internet reading that guys were attracted to the smell of pumpkin pie. She had learned about this aphrodisiac while researching Valentine's Day romance tips for the school paper. Her blog, *Uff Da*, had debuted at the beginning of the school year after she'd demonstrated her writing abilities with her investigative reports on the dwindling amount of fried cheese curds available in the cafeteria during lunch hour. She suspected that the deputy mayor had something to do with the problem—he usually was the person who ruined things at school. However, after bribing a few freshmen with custard shakes, Megan uncovered that the stoners had a deal with the lunch lady, who saved curds for them in exchange for some primo locally grown weed.

The stoners never came into the bait shop, but plenty of cute senior boys regularly shopped at Brabender's. It was only a matter of time. Granted, there were plenty of weird older men, too, but none worse than all the toothless guys who hung out at the Chitchat Supper Club and rehashed their grandfathers' tales of John Dillinger and Al Capone hiding in the Northwoods. Megan had been eating Friday fish fry there ever since she could remember, and she decided that the guys at the Chitchat and the bait shop were still a million times better than dealing with the vets who smoked outside the entrance to the Nimrod Lodge. Those Nimrod geezers always seemed to be in a competition to shout the creepiest comment to her as she walked past the building. So far, the winner in her mind was a tie between, "There she goes, Miss Almost Legal," and "Hey, looks like she's now a B-cup, I'm thinking!"

The Nimrod Lodge was a fraternal organization Bill Eckerstorfer created in northern Wisconsin around the turn of the century for hunting discussions and other manly things. These manly discussions continued into the 1960s when it became increasingly difficult to convince young men that being called a Nimrod was a hip, trendy addition to one's resume.

Nimrod was a perfectly fine name for a fraternal hunting lodge in 1901, when *nimrod* meant powerful and mighty hunter. The name came from a famous hunter in the Bible, a gamesman extraordinaire and the great-grandson of Noah—the guy who built the Ark! How manly! But over the course of the twentieth century, the word slowly evolved into meaning a dim-witted and idiotic person—not something that really appealed to teenage boys, unless it were in reference to the Green Day album. Women were finally allowed to join the Nimrod Lodge in 1979, and membership had stayed fairly high ever since, especially after the lodge subscribed to premium cable in order to get all those college football games.

On that particular Sunday morning in May, the Nimrod geezers were still smoking on the lodge's porch while Megan was dealing with a cute little girl who had spilled a container of earthworms. Megan gave her a fat worm that she'd picked off the floor. The girl grabbed it and squealed as it moved in her hand. She instinctively tossed it back to Megan. It promptly hit her square in the chest and slid down her cleavage.

With a resigned sigh, Megan reached into her bra and pulled out the slimy earthworm. She grabbed the jar of pumpkin pie spice from her nearby backpack and sprinkled some down her shirt. The spice stuck to the trail of slime and dirt on her skin.

"At least it matches the dirt, right?" Megan said to the puzzled little girl, who immediately ran to her mom.

"Hey, kid! Can we have a day's worth of minnows?" shouted a guy in his late thirties.

His friend chimed in, "And whatever you have that will land those monster muskies that you guys are so famous for."

Muskies, the prized muskellunge fish found deep within the lakes of northern Wisconsin, were the most sought-after trophy fish across the Northwoods. They could grow to more than fifty-five inches long and weigh nearly sixty pounds, providing an exhilarating fight to the angler lucky enough to get a strike. Fearsome predators, muskies could consume prey up to two-thirds of their body length, including muskrats and ducks. The musky was not only the official state fish but also the subject of most exaggerated fishing stories drunk men told at taverns across the state.

"Suckers," Megan began as she walked over to the register. "But Opening Day for muskies isn't until next weekend."

"Dude!" Bro Number Two yelled accusingly at Bro Number One. "You said opening day was last weekend!"

"Well, opening day was last weekend," offered Megan.

"So we can fish for muskies," said Bro Number One, who turned to Bro Number Two. "I told you."

"No, not until Opening Day this Friday," said Megan.

"But you just said opening day was last weekend," countered Bro Number Two. *This is one stupid girl*, he thought.

"Yeah, so you can fish for everything else," answered Megan. Unfortunately, neither bro could hear the difference in Megan's tone between *Opening Day* and *opening day*, which all Mistakers understood. The beginning of May meant opening day, when the lakes were open for all fishing except muskies. Musky fishing was always a week or two later, on Opening Day. All Mistakers, like Megan, verbally capitalized the day that musky fishing opened, because that was obviously much more important than fishing for walleyes, bluegills, or crappies. Megan didn't bother to explain. It was fun to mess with their heads since she was bored.

"Don't forget the six-packs, sweetheart!" yelled their other buddy. Bro Number Three was wearing a Chicago Bears baseball cap and wandering around holding up his smartphone in search of a Wi-Fi signal.

"You guys from Chicago?" she said with her most saccharine smile.

"Da Bears!" chanted all three friends in unison.

Nothing got under the skin of Mistakers quite like wealthy, vacationing Chicagoans, mainly because the locals were convinced that the Illinois tourists constantly took the best fish out of the water. These fish should belong to Mistakers, but the cool kids from Chicago gobbled them up instead. The cool kids already lived in an awesome cosmopolitan city. They didn't need to drive all the way up to Mistake to take things that weren't theirs.

That was kind of how Megan felt about her Svenson cousins who lived thirty minutes away in Poubelle. Poubelle was a fancy village that had grown from an old nineteeth-century French Canadian settlement. *Poubelle* was also the French word for garbage can, a fact that Megan always included when talking to her cousins about anything. Those garbage can Svensons had a newly built house (they built their house!), with a foyer, a balcony over the foyer, and an amazing, finished-off basement. Plus, they had a deck and a three-car garage. They didn't even need boat storage for the winter. So when Svenson cousins borrowed Megan's clothes and then returned them in terrible condition, well, it was annoying as heck.

That's how Mistakers felt about Chicagoans fishing in their backyard. "You already have the best prom dresses, the best pizza, and Oprah. Please don't take our fish and mount them above your fireplace. Or release them back into the lake with their guts ripped out because you don't know how to properly remove the hook."

Megan was certain that these overgrown frat boys had no idea what they were doing with the bait and tackle that they were buying from her. Bro Number Two high-fived Bro Number Three. "Yeah, just for you, my man! Schweitzman bachelor-party weekend in full force!"

Megan added a 20 percent douche bag surcharge to their purchase. The bros didn't even ask for the total and paid with a corporate card. No one ever paid for bait with a corporate account. Well, no one besides the Lake Mistake Country Club, which had a corporate deal with Brabender's in order to keep the boats of its well-heeled members fully stocked with worms and lures.

After signing their receipt, the bros strutted out of the store with their suckers, minnows, crankbaits, and beer, very excited to go musky fishing on the famous lakes of Mistake. Winter lingered with an unwelcome icy grip, but the air was finally warming up, and the ice was melting on at least one or two lakes in the extremely late spring thaw. Megan wasn't too concerned about their obvious illegal musky fishing goals. She knew that the Waumabenon County Sheriff's Department would take care of the fishermen bros from Chicago.

She took her phone out of her pocket and returned to studying a local news story about fourteen mailboxes, shaped like musky fish, that had disappeared from Mistake. A quote from Deputy Mayor Trollqvist jumped out at her: "The sheriff may not be able to comment on an ongoing investigation, but I certainly can. It's obviously teenagers, and they need to be stopped."

Ugh, of course the Troll blames us, Megan thought. *He's the one that needs to be stopped!* Megan had been trying for months to end the Troll's meddling at Mistake High School. She vowed to do everything she could to stop his interference once and for all.

As she continued reading, she took a deep breath of cinnamon, nutmeg, and minnows. *Still better than working with Mom or Dad at the custard stand.*

THREE

Svenson's Frozen Custard had been in Mistake since 1949, when Megan's grandfather opened the small shop next to the high school. Her parents, Todd and Cheryl, took over the business when she was little. The custard stand was so successful that Todd started a second location in 2000, the opening of which established him as one of the top ten entrepreneurs in Mistake since 1920s bootlegging.

The 1920s were Mistake's glory days. The town boomed so much during Prohibition that it was incorporated into a city during the Jazz Age. It was like the California Gold Rush—if the California Gold Rush had swarms of mosquitoes and severe thunderstorms. Chicago bootleggers took to Mistake like muskies to water. With a name like Mistake, their confidence in the level to which the tiny eight-man Waumabenon County Sheriff's Department (WCSD) cared about investigating anything was dead accurate. They didn't care at all. They were too busy quality-checking the new brothels on Main Street. The deputies were also helpful by misdirecting Hoover's G-men to speakeasies in other towns. When the Great Depression followed, it ravaged the rest of the country, but in Mistake, new businesses boomed, unemployment stayed low, and the number of taverns tripled thanks to the gangster money that flowed through the town during the previous decade of bootlegging lawlessness.

Years later, the WCSD stepped up policing in a big way when the city became overrun with Chicagoans of more disrepute in the 1960s: the weekend tourist, aka the Chicago-scumbag-who-is-going-to-take-all-the-muskies-out-of-the-lakes tourist. The sheriff's department immediately ramped up with a particular show of force by patrolling the lakes to measure the minimum size and weight of the muskies tourists caught. Then they completely looked the other way when those tourists got drunk later in the evening. The WCSD didn't want tourists emptying the lakes, but they sure welcomed all the kegs they bought and emptied.

Tourists also bought a lot of frozen custard, which is why Todd Svenson quadrupled the production of Blue Moon in the warmer months. It was always a popular flavor but especially during the summer, when loads of tourists wanted to find out just what the heck a pale Blue Moon tasted like. Todd's secret ingredient was using heavy cream soaked overnight in vats of fruit-flavored cereal. It was so much cheaper and tastier than spending money to buy flavor additives. Svenson's Blue Moon was renowned across the Northwoods as some of the finest in the Midwest, and people traveled all the way from Michigan's Upper

Peninsula for a taste. Svenson's was so popular that it was open 24-7 from April to September.

The shortest distance anyone traveled for Blue Moon was across the street. Some cops lived for donuts and coffee. Deputies in Mistake lived for either brandy old-fashioneds or frozen custard. Sheriff Lori Holm, Megan's aunt, liked frozen custard when she was on duty at WCSD headquarters. The department had imposed a strict no-indulging-before-ten-a.m. rule on custard after a dozen deputies got sick from an early morning binge in honor of the second Svenson's opening next to headquarters. In spite of the rule, both stands did brisk business with Mistake's finest, despite being only one mile apart.

It was because of that brisk business that the drive-through cashier, sophomore Taylor Helstrom, failed to notice the pile of musky mailboxes in the back of classmate Brett Brabender's pickup when Brett and his buddy, Gunnar Smith, stopped for Blue Moon shakes one Sunday at three a.m.

FOUR

It was just after ten a.m. on Sunday when Sheriff Lori Holm's phone rang as she tipped her dripping cone of frozen custard to her lips.

"*Uff da*," she grumbled as she recognized the mayor's number on the caller ID. She stared longingly at the Blue Moon custard and ignored the call. Svenson's only featured it as the flavor of the day twelve times per month, no matter how many times she begged her brother-in-law, Todd, to offer it more. She managed to devour half the custard by the time her grouchy fifty-six-year-old assistant, Mike Zwicky, opened her door and barked that there'd been more crime. Like all crotchety old people, Mike spent most of the day complaining that the younger generation was ruining America with their electronic devices, optimism, and viral cat videos.

"You'd better get over to Loon Hollow," said Mike. "Those little punks are at it again."

Sheriff Holm pulled into Loon Hollow, a neighborhood near the elementary school in the old part of town. It was full of cozy homes, large yards, and, depending on the season, an angry flock of wild turkeys that taunted the local dog population. Deputy Andy Svingen, so handsome that he looked straight out of central casting, greeted her upon arrival. "They got this whole street. All of the musky mailboxes except for Mrs. Larson's."

Makes sense, thought Sheriff Holm. The neighborhood mail carrier frequently filed complaints about the height and thickness of the shrubbery surrounding Mrs. Larson's mailbox. Delivery of her mail was a daily triumph for the US Postal Service, so there's no way a group of drunk teenagers would be dedicated enough to hack through that brush.

"That's an even two dozen in the past four days," she said.

"Hi, Aunt Lori!" Megan said as she appeared next to Deputy Svingen.

"Morning! Oh, hey, got your e-mail. Tuesday at the Chitchat sounds good."

"Great. It should be a fun birthday night for Mom."

"How's your Opening Day planning going, Megan?" Deputy Svingen asked. "Gonna be in any competitions?"

"Maybe. I have to help at the custard stand that Dad is setting up by the lake, so I don't know." Megan gestured to an empty mailbox post. "How many more did they get last night?"

"Looks like ten."

"All from Loon Hollow? Do you have any leads?"

"Don't you worry about it, Megan. Your aunt will get them."

"I know she will." Megan smiled at her aunt. *But who knows what the Troll will do before then,* she thought. "Anything I can do to help? I already asked Lina and my parents if they saw anything last night. Nothing."

"Sheriff! Sheriff!" Mayor Ole Oland rushed over—lumbered, really. He was fat in that weird-uncle kind of way.

Sheriff Holm rolled her eyes under her dark sunglasses. "Sir."

"Sheriff, did you hear?"

"Yes, sir. That's why I'm here." *You big idiot.*

Mayor Ole had been reelected two years ago in a landslide. Mistakers called him by his first name because three of the last four mayors were Olands. Being mayor was the Oland family business. Mayor Ole's opponent, Ryan Bossy, presented concrete ideas on how to improve the local logging industry and reduce drunk snowmobiling. Mayor Ole offered to extend bar hours by an hour. After losing the election, Bossy moved to Madison, where he became a successful lobbyist for the alcohol industry. In the end, it was still a win-win for Mistake.

"Did anyone see anything unusual this time?" asked Sheriff Holm as she looked around.

Ignoring her, Mayor Ole barked, "We need a task force. We have to get to the bottom of this before the tourists find out. Nearly thirty muskies are gone!"

"Sir, I don't think tourists will stop visiting Mistake because of a few stolen mailboxes."

"Musky mailboxes, sheriff! Musky mailboxes. What's Mistake without muskies?" Mayor Ole looked at Sheriff Holm, Megan, and Deputy Svingen for an answer.

Megan just shrugged and said, "Swedetown?"

In addition to the fishing tourism, the musky was also the mascot of the high school and, therefore, Mistake. The musky was the reason why the city was named Mistake so many years ago. Back in the late eighteen hundreds, the men in charge of Swedetown needed to pick an all-American name for the postmark of the newly established post office. So they voted on the name Mistake, thinking it was a great way to deter anyone from moving to the area. Heaven forbid they deplete the bountiful musky population.

The irony was lost on the city council nearly one hundred years later when it launched a huge tourism campaign to lure visitors based on the musky fishing. So Mistake chugged along into the new millennium powered by everything musky, from musky mailboxes to the Musky Slide, the world's largest—and only—musky waterslide. The souvenir business was also strong, with heavy sales of slogan T-shirts, the most popular of which were baby onesies like "I'm the mistake from Mistake, Wisconsin," and "Whoops! My parents went to Mistake, Wisconsin."

But no matter how much Mistakers of all ages loved muskies, that still didn't stop teenagers from being idiots after a few beers.

"I'll give you a holler with the details, sheriff. We'll hold a press conference on the Musky Mailbox Task Force this afternoon," wheezed an out-of-breath Mayor Ole as he lurched away.

"I'll be there, Mayor Ole! I'll cover it for the school paper!" Megan yelled after him. She turned to her aunt. "I'll see you this afternoon. Gotta go get ready." She ran back inside to prepare for her very first press conference. She hoped that the Troll would be there—she had a few questions for him.

Sheriff Holm rolled her eyes again. *What a waste of time.* There were only a few days to nab people fishing illegally for muskies. All of those people would be tourists, most of whom had also failed to buy a fishing license from the Wisconsin Department of Natural Resources. It was a rare two-for-one tourist-crackdown opportunity. The WCSD had just purchased three new boats, bringing the total number of boats to nine, for the sole purpose of catching (Chicago) tourists without licenses. Fishing without a license was the most highly enforced crime in Mistake.

The second most-enforced law was snowmobile speeding, followed by enforcement of a state law that barred construction of new boathouses on lakes across the Badger State. The sheriff was always surprised by the number of people who tried to get around that one. Her favorite excuse was that aliens came down from outer space and built the boathouse during the middle of the night. Being a more intelligent species and all, the aliens also apparently had the foresight to pay off the neighbors with good old American dollars to ignore the construction.

FIVE

Boathouses were certainly on the Troll's mind. He was the kind of guy who took pride in his nickname—at least he did now. He didn't much like hearing it shouted at him back in seventh-grade gym class, when he was trying to complete the President's Challenge fitness test. Even though it was a pretty obvious nickname for someone born as Kenny Trollqvist, he took pride in knowing that someday he'd prove he wasn't the lame troll of his school days in neighboring Waunomonee. He'd finally have all the power, money, and influence that he'd always sought.

Soon, Mistake's Deputy Mayor Kenny "the Troll" Trollqvist would have the special permit that he needed to begin construction on his new boathouse.

Having a boathouse guaranteed popularity, and the Troll desperately wanted to be popular. But lake homes with boathouses rarely went on the market, and if they did, they were way out of the Troll's price range. *Goddamn DNR*, he seethed. *It's my God-given right as an American to build a boathouse!* The Wisconsin Department of Natural Resources didn't see it that way.

State law prohibited construction of new boathouses extending over the water if the structure were built completely or partially below the ordinary high watermark, i.e., the boundary between the publicly owned lake and the privately owned land. The law protected the shoreline, wildlife habitats, and water quality—things most people cared about. Of course, the Troll thought this was complete political BS. All the cool boathouses were built below the watermark so that you could drive your boat right into its little garage after a long day of fishing and then party on the second level.

Boathouses built before the law's enactment in the late 1970s were grandfathered in, making them extremely valuable. Homeowners with grandfathered boathouses usually kept them in the family, and those lucky enough to have two-story boathouses, like the Eckerstorfer family, always hosted the most-talked-about summer parties.

Well, this year, the Troll was finally going to be one of those people. He had discovered a way to get approval for a building permit for the shiny new boathouse of his dreams. Soon he would have a series of the most-exclusive boathouse parties anyone in Mistake—heck, all of Waumabenon County—had ever seen.

He'd also finally get rid of that annoying loon nest along his shoreline. He hated those damn birds and their awful shrieking calls. Tourists to the Northwoods romanticized loon calls as haunting. The Troll described the calls as freaking annoying. The common loon was a beloved bird not only in Wisconsin but also in neighboring Minnesota, where it enjoyed official status as the state bird. He was pleased that the state bird of Wisconsin was the hardworking robin, not that wailing water bird with the devil-red eyes.

Soon enough, the obnoxious loons would be gone. All he had to do to get his special boathouse permit was obtain a building permit for a Chicago company, Whole Lotta Bait, to build its first bait shop in Mistake. Easy. He didn't like to use the word *illegal* to describe either permit. *Special*, that's what he called them. The Troll didn't see this as taking a bribe. No, this whole thing was just an exchange of building permits between Americans who had the right to build whatever they wanted. Besides, the lot that Whole Lotta Bait wanted was vacant, anyway. In fact, it had just been razed, a coincidence that the Troll believed was a cosmic blessing to his plans.

SIX

A Chicago-based Midwest empire, Whole Lotta Bait was more famous for its in-store bars with hot waitresses, the Whole Lotta Girls, than the quality of the live bait it sold to fishermen. Don and Scottie Kaczmarski, two best friends and kinda-dumb cousins from Chicago Central High School, founded Whole Lotta Bait in the mid-2000s.

The concept came to the Kaczmarskis after they took a trip to New York to celebrate finally graduating high school as fifth-year seniors. The Urban Woodsman Workshop in Times Square inspired the Whole Lotta Bait combo of fishing and hot girls. That store in midtown appealed to tourists who genuinely liked woodwork, as well as wannabe hipsters who aspired to be Paul Bunyan with a manicure. But most important, it also appealed to every horny teenager and finance bro who wandered past the store. Aside from the working woodshop, an array of expensive wooden toys that kids didn't want (but moms thought were so pretty), and a variety of two-by-fours for sale, the main draws were the sexy lady lumberjacks serving craft beer.

Even with their beer goggles (courtesy of their fake IDs), the Kaczmarski cousins saw their crystal-clear future after ten pints of overpriced wet-hop IPA. They were thrilled when they realized they could combine fishing, boobs, and beer as a successful business. Upon their return to Chicago, they immediately hung up their official Urban Woodsman calendar of lady lumberjacks and scribbled their business plan for Whole Lotta Bait on the back of a week-old pizza box. Their main selling points were hot Whole Lotta Girls serving cheap beer at the Tall Tales Speakeasy inside a bait emporium where dudes could swap fishing tips and fantasy hookup stories.

The Kaczmarskis came from wealthy families, so money, permits, bribes, and supplies were no problem. The original store opened in 2005 near the Fox Chain O'Lakes in northern Illinois, and the guys couldn't believe the 1,000 percent markup on worms. The second location opened one year later. The business grew exponentially after that, like one of those shapes the cousins had learned about in algebra class—or they would have learned about if they hadn't paid David Davidson to do all of their math homework. Coincidentally, they also now paid him to be their CFO, perhaps the first documented case of an exploited former nerd triumphing in partnership with his former exploiters.

Because of the booming Whole Lotta Bait franchise, a kitschy, old store in Mistake named Artsy Loon had recently gone out of business. It was a real bummer for Megan and her friends because it had been their hangout since elementary school. They loved sitting at the old soda fountain and drinking freshly mixed cherry sodas. Megan blogged about the Artsy Loon on *Uff Da* in an effort to save it, but it was of no use. The store was razed, and the land was purchased by Intermediary Development Group, LLC. If anyone had bothered to look at the paperwork, he would have discovered that Intermediary Development Group, LLC, had purchased Artsy Loon for seventeen times its value, sending the owners into blissful retirement in Costa Rica.

The owners had been paid off before Whole Lotta Bait even secured the services of the Troll. Whole Lotta Bait knew it would take months to win over the city council to obtain a legal building permit, given the hostile environment in Mistake toward Chicago businesses. Luckily, they had been tipped off about the Troll's ability to be a semicompetent fixer in a position of power. It was pretty easy for Whole Lotta Bait to figure out the carrot to dangle in front of him, because one quick Internet search revealed his obsession with boathouses and his American right to build one right over those freaking loons.

The land for the new store, located next to the Musky Slide, didn't even need to be rezoned. Whole Lotta Bait just needed the key building permit, which the Troll promised to deliver to three of the Kaczmarskis' most-trusted marketing men. As for the all-important liquor license, Whole Lotta Bait had that within five minutes of searching online. Legal liquor licenses in Mistake took a simple two-step online process with instant approval. The five-dollar license fee went to local charities. Nearly everything in Mistake was licensed for liquor, including Lutheran churches. They did a brisk Sunday-football beer business except in the depths of winter, when snowstorms usually kept Packers fans confined to indoor neighborhood parties. If they were lucky, they landed at one of the parties in the legendary basement at the Brabenders' house.

SEVEN

The Brabenders lived in Loon Hollow. Being in the old part of town, it was a classic midcentury neighborhood with a pleasant mix of ranch and two-story homes with no McMansions in sight. The Brabender boys were the kind of kids that people endured, especially their next-door neighbors, the Svensons. The boys were all named after famous people from the Green Bay Packers, carrying on the tradition started with their dad, Bart Starr Brabender. Brett Favre Brabender was the oldest at sixteen. Vince Lombardi Brabender was twelve, and identical twins Curly Lambeau Brabender and Reggie White Brabender were nine. When referring to their children as a group, Mrs. Brabender called them "the boys." They were always "the Hall of Famers" to Bart. Someday he hoped to have a grandson named Aaron Rodgers Brabender.

Bart loved fishing, which is why he started his successful bait business just before he got married. Brabender's Bait was one of the most popular live-bait shops in Mistake because of its appeal to sports fans. A couple of years ago, a second-string Packers player stopped by and bought a container of earthworms and three scoops of minnows. Bart immediately hung a photo of the Packer on the wall, and the player became more famous in Mistake for shopping at Brabender's than for anything from his bench-warming career. There was a spike in customers soon afterward, because no one wanted to miss any other football players. But even before that random player bought worms, Brabender's had been known as a place where football fans could play Monday-morning quarterback after learning the day's fishing news.

While her husband gossiped away at the bait shop, Mrs. Brabender was a second-grade teacher who put all of her effort into her job and was then just too tired to work when she got home—at least, that was the theory held by the neighbors that her children slightly terrorized. Brett was the ringleader, like most older brothers, but Vince and the Toxic Twins were also strategic in their attempts at chaos. The neighborhood moms and dads never knew which twin was responsible for drawing chalk penises on the driveways, and there were only so many times they could complain about a kid they couldn't identify 100 percent. To be fair, the Brabenders were never that horrible, especially compared to the Eckerstorfers or the Bjorlings. Now, those kids were destined for jail.

In the end, people liked Mr. and Mrs. Brabender enough that the neighborhood was convinced there was hope for the kids yet. But no one wanted to babysit them.

The worst part for the kids of Loon Hollow and their parents was that the Brabenders had the best finished-off basement in the neighborhood. Finished-off basements were second only to boathouses in Mistake in terms of the cool factor for parties. The Brabenders' basement was decorated with stuffed deer and musky trophies, a pool table, a stocked bar, and a large flat-screen TV with the latest gaming system. To adults, the phrase "the Brabenders are having a party" was met with excitement and dread. Mom and Dad would get to attend a boozy Sunday football party, but their son might end up with a dick drawn on his face with permanent marker if the Toxic Twins grabbed him during halftime. Every Brabender party ended with a check of the Brabender family boat, because that's where moms and dads would find their missing children. Anyone that Brett deemed annoying was usually trapped belowdecks during the course of the party. Brett had trapped Megan there once, and she refused to go to Brabender parties ever since.

Right now, the only things in the Brabenders' boat were fourteen stolen musky mailboxes underneath the tarp. The ten stolen from Loon Hollow on Saturday night were still in the pickup. The mailboxes all basically looked the same, with a fish body as the box, a fin for the flag, and a hinged mouth that served as the opening. Each musky mailbox also had huge, gleaming, glow-in-the-dark eyes that scared any out-of-towner driving through Mistake in the evening.

As he sat in bed that Sunday morning, Brett tried to figure out what to do with them. Opening Day was coming up, and his dad was going to want to use the truck tomorrow for work and use the boat on Friday. His friend Gunnar had wanted to smash them with a bat, but Brett wanted them in one piece in case he had any ideas. He usually had pretty good ideas. In fact, he'd already had an awesome idea for the one with the name *Helstrom* painted on the side, which is why it was the first mailbox that he stole.

He thought back to how easy it had been. He waited until he saw Mrs. Helstrom turn off the lights and go to bed. He walked over, detached the mailbox, and hid it inside the Brabender boat. The next morning he sat on his front porch and watched Mrs. Helstrom, wearing a robe and fuzzy loon slippers, wander to the curb to get the morning paper. When she saw that her mailbox was missing, she screamed, "Mr. Postie!" Much to the chagrin of her kids, Mrs. Helstrom affectionately referred to her musky mailbox as Mr. Postie the Musky.

She was about to run inside to call the WCSD when she noticed that Sheriff Holm was standing in the Svensons' driveway, talking to Megan before heading to headquarters. Mrs. Helstrom screamed, "Sheriff Holm! Sheriff Holm! Mr. Postie! He's gone!" She ran across the street and grabbed the sheriff's arm.

"What does he look like?" Sheriff Holm asked.

"He has lovely big eyes. Kind eyes. And he's about this big," Mrs. Helstrom said as she held her hands two feet apart.

"What's the breed?"

"Breed? I don't know!" Mrs. Helstrom shrieked. "I didn't know they had breeds!" She started to hyperventilate. "Mr. Postie! Mr. Postie, where are you?"

"Don't worry about specifics, Mrs. Helstrom. But are we talking poodle or lab or retriever?"

"We're talking musky," Megan said.

"What the heck kind of dog is that?"

"Not a missing dog. Mr. Postie is the name of her musky mailbox," Megan said as she rolled her eyes. "It's just her mailbox."

"And he's gone!" Mrs. Helstrom wailed as she crumpled into the grass.

Brett laughed at the memory. It had been pretty funny to observe the scene unfolding a few days ago. Brett remembered watching Megan trying not to giggle as her aunt was forced into awkwardly consoling Mrs. Helstrom. Thinking about Megan's scrunched up face made him smile.

EIGHT

The Svensons still had their musky mailbox, which was good news for Nielsen's, a Midwest clothing store whose entire marketing strategy depended upon the availability of mailboxes for daily delivery of 15-percent-off coupons. The Nielsen's coupon receptacle was next to the newspaper box, both of which were mounted on a wooden post that was a prime destination stop for the family dog, Brandy, when he accompanied Todd to collect the morning newspaper.

The latest edition of *The Waumabenon Times* sat on the Svensons' kitchen table that Sunday as Brandy snoozed in the corner after completing his important morning task. Megan wandered into the kitchen, flopped into a chair at the table, and began flipping through the paper in search of pictures from the Mistake High baseball game.

"Is there any coffee left?" she asked.

"Not for you," her mom, Cheryl, answered.

"Why can't I ever have any coffee?"

"Because it will stunt your growth," Cheryl responded with her usual stock answer. She was standing in front of the open freezer, chipping away with a screwdriver at food that had frozen together.

"Ugh, no, it won't."

"Yes, it will. Melanie Chevalier said so on the news." A box of waffles broke free and flew out of the freezer, landing on the floor. "*Uff da*," said Cheryl, pointing at them with the screwdriver. "You wanna eat those, Megan?"

"But I didn't sleep at all last night," Megan argued as she searched for the waffle box that had slid under the table.

"You're not getting any coffee." Cheryl continued to chip away at a package of vegetables that was frozen to a quart of custard. With a loud thwack, the vegetables broke free and fell to the floor.

As Cheryl bent over to pick them up, she noticed the time on her watch and yelled over her shoulder, "Lina! Get outta bed! It's nearly lunch! Remember, you're cleaning the bathroom today!"

Lina answered from upstairs, "That's real good motivation, Mom!"

"Lina!"

"I'm coming!"

Megan picked up the waffles, opened the box, and put one in the toaster. Still looking in vain for sympathy in her quest for coffee, she added, "Stupid Brett came home at three fifteen in the morning. So, of course, he woke me up with his dumb speakers in his truck."

Megan and Brett had a long, rocky history together. It was the kind of love-hate relationship that only kids of the same age and opposite sex who were forced to live next door to each other for most of their lives could have. In kindergarten, Brett had stabbed Megan with a huge thorn that he'd ripped off a tree branch because she'd hit a baseball farther than he could. An hour later, they'd played pirates with their siblings in the Brabenders' impressive Swiss Family Robinson-like tree house. By the time first grade rolled around, Brett regularly stopped by Megan's house to borrow copies of the adventure book series *The Chronicles of the Kinockina Lake Gang*, and they'd discuss their favorite parts on the school bus the next day.

Their peaceful play abruptly ended in second grade when Brett missed a week of school because of chicken pox. When he returned, the entire class found out that Megan had been bringing homework over to his house. Naturally, they immediately chanted, "Megan loves Brett." Megan had turned bright red out of embarrassment because she most definitely did not have a crush on stupid Brett.

"No, I don't," was all she could manage before running to the girls' bathroom.

Meanwhile, as a defense mechanism, Brett had launched into a comedy routine about how she was a terrible girlfriend. The routine mostly included jokes from *Single Sergio*, a long-running sitcom that his dad liked and his mom loathed.

Megan hated Brett afterward, and for years, he made it a point to make fun of her all the time at school. He didn't want to disappoint his adoring audience.

He even managed to ruin the famous Musky Slide every summer during middle school. The Musky Slide was built when they were little kids to commemorate the seventy-fifth anniversary of the incorporation of Mistake. Erected on a hill, the incredibly simple but popular waterslide comprised a giant, lifelike, fiberglass musky built on top of a fifty-yard length of ten-foot-wide plastic boat covering that stretched from the top of the hill to the bottom. Dozens of garden hoses poured water onto the plastic at the top of the slide, near the musky's mouth. It was basically a huge poor man's Slip 'N Slide down a hill with a musky tunnel placed on top of it so that kids could slide through the fish after a running start on the hilltop. Even though the slide was no-frills, children across the Northwoods loved it, especially after the cotton candy truck started parking at the bottom of the hill.

When the city council originally proposed the slide, Mrs. "Don't Call Me Judy" Helstrom led a massive community debate among moms about how it was offensive to slide into the fish's mouth and be pooped out the butt. As a mom, she was outraged. The debate raged until someone reminded the moms that the structure's basic idea was to slide through an entire musky, so the only other option was to enter through the butt and be vomited out the mouth. Mrs. Helstrom and the other outraged moms hadn't thought about that.

As usual, they'd forgotten that kids would be thrilled to line up at the musky's mouth to let gravity take them through the animal from head to tail. Boys absolutely loved referring to riding the slide as "getting pooped." Moms always forget about these basic kid things when they get outraged. Nearly all teenage boys who vacationed in Mistake bought T-shirts that said, "I got pooped in Mistake, Wisconsin." The shirts were even favorites among locals like the Brabender boys.

Megan and her friends also enjoyed using the waterslide multiple times on a hot summer day, except for the times that Brett somehow managed to sneak in immediately behind her. He'd crash into her at the bottom with such spectacular force that she'd shoot off the boat plastic and into the grass, where she'd get covered in grass stains and mud. She knew his buddies manned the top of the slide as their summer job, but she never knew that her sister tipped off Brett when she'd head over to the slide with friends. Lina happily made the deal in exchange for public attention from Brett at school, where he began acknowledging her presence in the hall. Brett noticed that the more jock nods he gave her in the hallway, the more puppy-love favors she'd do for him, like coupons for free Svenson's Frozen Custard or saving his place in the long lunch line on taquito day.

Unfortunately, the Musky Slide was currently out of commission. A few months ago, a drunk snowmobiler from Waunomonee had the brilliant idea to drive through the slide, even though it was fenced off for the winter season. Not surprisingly, since there was a fence in place, he crashed into the mouth of the slide and destroyed the entrance. The Nimrod Lodge had been raising funds to repair the damaged fiberglass fish at its free monthly gun safety classes for teens.

They were still a few hundred short after lodge leaders had to raid the donations to repair the Nimrod's front porch after a gun lesson went awry.

The broken slide certainly put a kink in Lina's plans for accumulating additional social capital via jock nods at school, even though Brett didn't seem to be crashing into Megan as much anymore. Lina's unrequited crush on Brett had raged for the past several years, ever since he appeared in a local print ad for his dad's bait shop. The ad featured a photo of Brett hoisting a giant musky over his head, which nicely showed off his newly acquired muscles. She had pinned it to her bulletin board and frequently found herself losing thought when she was supposed to be doing homework. After a long dreamy stare at the photo that morning, Lina finally moped into the kitchen wearing her pajamas.

"It's alive!" teased Megan.

"Shut up," Lina grumbled as she cut a slice of the almond kringle sitting on the counter. "What time are we going to lutefisk supper tonight?"

"No, we're having chicken tonight," Cheryl said.

"We have to go!"

Megan rolled her eyes. "What, is Brett going?"

"Shut up!"

"The chicken's going to go bad otherwise. We need to eat it."

"Yummy, nearly expired chicken," Megan said as she struggled to spread cold butter on her toaster waffle. "Served with a side of salmonella."

"Then drop me off at church. I have to go," Lina demanded.

"No, you don't. You have to go clean the bathroom and sort through that box of clothes that's been sitting in the hall all week," Cheryl said as she continued to chip away at the frozen food. "We can go next week."

"You're ruining my life!" Lina yelled as she stormed out of the kitchen, furiously typing on her phone. Since she was completely occupied with telling everyone online that her mom was being epically unfair, she didn't see the package of frozen chicken that had flown out of the freezer. She slipped on it, landed on the floor, and realized that she had accidentally liked a photo posted by her dumb sister.

"No!" she shrieked as she threw the frozen thighs at Megan. "Stupid chicken!"

NINE

This is wonderful, Mayor Ole thought as he peeked out from behind the pink curtain that was hanging temporarily in the City Hall conference room. Even though it was pink, the curtain was perfect. It definitely lent a sense of grand occasion to the proceedings. He had seen his assistant, Alexis Akerbladh, roll her eyes when he told her to drop what she was doing and run to the Nielsen's down the road to buy a bedsheet. He didn't understand what she didn't understand about the ceremony of a press conference as important as the one he was about to conduct.

"Something dark, nothing white. Take petty cash. Here's a Nielsen's coupon," he had barked as he'd pulled her chair away from her desk, ignoring that Alexis was still in the chair, holding a cup of coffee, and connected to her computer by a pair of expensive headphones wrapped around her neck. As Mayor Ole quickly rolled her to the door, her coffee spilled onto her new skirt when the headphone cord became taut. "And for Pete's sake, wear something clean. I shouldn't even have to say that, you know."

Oh, I'll wear something clean, thought Alexis as she grabbed some twenties from petty cash. *Something around the forty-dollar range.*

This was Mayor Ole's third press conference about a task force since he'd been elected. That was three more than all other Mistake mayors combined. He created the first task force after the annual spring junior-senior prank wars. His house was egged even though his kids weren't old enough to be in high school. He'd ranted to the local media that "kids today have no respect," and "they need the swift, full justice of the law."

Four hours later, the task force was disbanded after Sheriff Holm reported her findings. Ole's own middle-school children had borrowed eggs from some juniors and egged their house to protest their dad's new curfew rules. The mayor immediately labeled the findings as classified and distracted the local media with the announcement of a new fishing contest for Opening Day.

Mayor Ole reluctantly established the second task force at the demand of City Hall employees, who were angry and hungry because their lunches kept disappearing from the shared refrigerator. After the task force installed hidden cameras in the kitchen, in spite of the mayor's strong protest on privacy grounds, no sandwich ever went missing again. The case remained unsolved, although Mayor Ole seemed to lose ten pounds.

Now, his announcement of the third task force was imminent. The small conference room buzzed with excitement as more people arrived. Ole couldn't wait for his moment in the spotlight. In his opinion, he was zero-for-two in successful task forces, but that was finally going to change.

Across the room, the Troll greeted the invited members of the media, which was everyone he could think of, from the TV station Lake News 37 to the church-bulletin lady to the guy who wrote the specials on the board outside of Tomahawk Coffee. The only person who didn't come was a reporter from the high school paper because she had a strict policy of not working on the weekends unless it involved the boys' soccer team. The coffee-specials guy wasn't quite sure why he was there, but he'd said yes because the Troll promised free kringle.

The Troll smiled to himself as he watched everyone devour the Danish kringle, the official state pastry of Wisconsin. He was thrilled to get rid of all the damned school-fundraiser kringle that he was pressured into buying from pushy moms at the office who were selling on behalf of their lazy children. He was also pleased at the hysteria he'd created surrounding the to-be-announced task force. The more the nosy reporters were distracted by the task force, the less time they had to dig around asking questions about the razed lot or the approved building permit in his pocket for Whole Lotta Bait. It only took eleven minutes of lingering around the city council reception desk buying kringle before he could slyly grab the "approved" stamp for the permit. Nineteen kringles was a small price to pay, even if he had to spend all that time inhaling the receptionist's horrible grandma perfume.

Suddenly, the Troll spotted Megan Svenson. He gritted his teeth and immediately walked over to her. "What are you doing here?"

"Hello, Troll," Megan said, her voice dripping with contempt. "I'm here to cover this for the school paper. You know, my blog."

"Oh, I'm well aware of your blog, Megan. But this is invite-only. And I didn't invite you."

"No. But Mayor Ole did." Megan waved to Mayor Ole, who was peeking out from behind the bedsheet. "Hey, Mayor Ole!" Mayor Ole excitedly returned the wave.

Megan turned back to the Troll. "See? And if you have any other questions about me being here, I'm sure my aunt, Sheriff Holm, can help you."

The Troll took a deep, angry breath. "Just sit down." He turned around and looked at his watch. It was go time. He nodded to Sheriff Holm, who was standing near the front of the room eating almond kringle and playing with her phone. He nodded to Mayor Ole, who was still peeking around the pink bedsheet featuring the cartoon of Mistake High's mascot, Mattie the Musky. The Troll wasn't quite sure what the task force's connection was to Mattie, especially since the mascot hadn't been stolen, but he figured it would certainly aid in distracting the reporters. Mayor Ole gave him a thumbs-up as he bit into a large piece of cherry kringle.

The Troll walked to the podium. "My fellow Mistakers, thanks for coming in on a Sunday for a very important and urgent message. Please get the word out there with all of your media. You've for sure heard about the awful thefts of our beloved musky mailboxes. Perhaps you've even been victimized by these jerks. Perhaps you're next on their list. With that in mind, may I introduce Mayor Ole," the Troll said as he applauded and backed away from the mic.

Mayor Ole began to speak. He had just enough cherry in the corners of his mouth to be distracting. "Thank you, Deputy Mayor Trollqvist. Folks, this musky mailbox thievery is an affront to everything that we hold dear. It's just beyond the pale. We must stop them. Not only for the good of our community, but for the tourists who come here to see our musky pride. These thieves need to be brought to justice before the innocence of our children is completely gone."

The Troll smiled. Mayor Ole was delivering his speech beautifully. He had sexed up the mayor's original announcement with words that all those cable news channels used to make things sound important. He told the mayor this would give his words the majesty they needed for a press conference with a curtain.

Mayor Ole continued while gesturing with kringle in his hand. "Our community hasn't been so terrorized since the Fourth of July chipmunk infestation of 1974. For Pete's sake, what message are we sending if we let these musky terrorists win? For the sake of our city, for the sake of our children, for the sake of the tourists who spend money in our city, I am announcing the establishment of the Musky Mailbox Task Force. Effective immediately, the full weight of the Waumabenon County Sheriff's Department will be used to investigate these awful crimes. Rescuing those mailboxes is the number-one priority for Sheriff Holm."

Sheriff Holm, who wasn't really listening, looked up from her phone when she heard her name. Realizing that no answer was required of her, she nodded at Mayor Ole and went back to texting her boyfriend, Justin Ranfranz, that perhaps they should just buy a new toaster even though he was sure he could fix the old one. Justin liked to fix a lot of things in their house, but this always ended up with Sheriff Holm actually repairing leaks, lights, and breaks after Justin poked the broken appliance with a screwdriver for three minutes and then went drinking with the boys. As a result, watching a lot of DIY TV became part of her life, which she really resented. She would much rather spend her free time watching reality shows about ridiculous rich women screaming at one another.

After pointing out Sheriff Holm to the press conference attendees, Mayor Ole paused and looked into the one camera that was recording. "We will find you." Then he shoved the last piece of kringle into his mouth. "You betcha."

Nailed it! The Troll was so pleased with himself that he nearly high-fived Mayor Ole as he stepped back up to the podium. "Any questions?"

Megan immediately stood up. "Megan Svenson, from Mistake High. When will students be allowed to sit in the luxury box at football games? The one you made us pay for. Without our consent."

"Megan, this isn't for questions about football."

"Then how much money have you made in kickbacks from changing the cafeteria lunch menu?"

"Do you have a question about the musky mailboxes?"

She didn't. She didn't really care about the missing mailboxes. She just wanted to put the Troll on the spot, in public, with questions that every teenager wanted him to answer. After thinking for a couple seconds she asked, "Well, are you getting a kickback from that too? I wouldn't be surprised."

"Anyone else have a question about the missing mailboxes?"

"So you have no comment?"

"No."

"Interesting," Megan said. As she sat down, other reporters began firing their questions at the Troll.

"Do you think it's teens from Waunomonee?"

"Is Mattie the Musky OK?"

"How do you know it's not the return of the chipmunks?"

"Should we steal Wally, the Waunomonee Walleye, as retaliation?"

"Did you know that Tomahawk Coffee has free refills after five p.m.?"

"How many chipmunks do you reckon it takes to carry one mailbox?"

"Will adults be able to trick-or-treat this year?"

"Any more cherry kringle?"

After ten minutes of questions, most of which turned into a planning session in the event that the chipmunks were hatching an anniversary attack, the Troll ended the press conference. "Thank you for your time, folks. All tips for the Musky Mailbox Task Force can go directly to Sheriff Holm, day or night. For the safety of all residents, for the pride of Mistake—heck, for America—make sure you leave no stone unturned in helping us find justice for these youthful hooligans. God bless Mistake."

As soon as the last piece of kringle was consumed, the Troll slipped out the back to change clothes. He had a date down by Waushauna Lake to swap permits with the guys from Whole Lotta Bait. It probably meant missing lutefisk dinner, but he could go next week.

TEN

The pungent smell of lutefisk hung in the air at Mistake Lutheran Church (ELCA) on Cranberry Road. Most sane people would gag at such a horrible smell and seriously question the cooking abilities of the chef. Then upon being served the fish, they'd probably think they were part of an Internet prank video. "So you're telling me that this colorless blob of smelly goo is supposed to be codfish? Ha-ha, you almost had me! Where's the camera? Did I win a boat?" The gross smell and booger-like consistency would finally make sense when they learned that lutefisk was the staple food of Vikings.

Somehow the turn-of-the-first-millennium recipe—which included reconstituting dried cod in lye—became part of the modern-day Scandinavian American experience. This fondness for lutefisk made no sense to anyone else, especially considering that lye had been a popular chemical in cleaning products since pioneer days. Frontier women used to mix it with wood ashes to make soap. But to residents with Scandinavian heritage in North Dakota, Minnesota, and Wisconsin, lutefisk was the smell of nostalgia and community. Those ties were so deep that the State of Wisconsin specifically exempted lutefisk as a toxic substance in Section 101.58 (2)(j)2.f of the Employees' Right to Know Law.

Despite its appearance and smell, everyone at Mistake Lutheran always took a big serving of lutefisk at the suppers. The hardiest of Mistakers (i.e., everyone who wore traditional Norwegian folk costumes known as *bunad*) cleaned their plates and made sure everyone knew it. Others drenched the lutefisk in melted butter so it slid down faster, but most threw it in the garbage after a ceremonial bite. Luckily, there was also a huge supply of delicious meatballs, vegetables, and Jansson's temptation, a traditional Swedish casserole made with potatoes, cream, and anchovies that tasted a heck of a lot better than it sounded. Desserts included a spread of cookies and *lefse*, which was basically a potato flatbread smeared with butter and brown sugar, then rolled into a perfect-sized sugar-delivery vehicle.

That Sunday evening in the fellowship hall, the Brabender boys spent dinner as they always did—challenging one another to tolerate lutefisk. Brett held the record for eating the largest serving without gagging, a feat that he had accomplished six months ago. Curly was currently sitting with his head inches from the plate, his hood pulled over his head to trap the lutefisk fumes in a game they called stink hood.

"Only thirteen more seconds!" Reggie shouted to his twin as Vince timed him on his phone.

Curly jerked his head up and inhaled a large breath. "I can't! I can't!" he gasped.

"Brett still has it by seven seconds!" exclaimed Vince. "You had to breathe like a little girl."

"Hey, you haven't even done stink hood since Christmas!" Curly said.

"Who cares about stink hood? I've been vomit champ since Thanksgiving."

Up until last November, the game was to eat a whole serving of lutefisk without puking. Usually Brett or Vince won, since their tolerance was highest. But then the boys realized it was a million times more fun to watch one another puke their guts out at church, so the game changed, and the winner was whoever hurled first. Vince was reigning champ, thanks to his ability to puke easily, which he always found helpful when he wanted to get out of a math test or impress new kids at school.

"Yeah, well, that's about to change," Brett said. He was annoyed that his younger brother had out-vomited him since New Year's Day. He figured he had a lock on it this time because he'd picked the grossest scoop of lutefisk he could find. He could feel the pre-puke saliva building up in his mouth just looking at the giant blob in front of him. "Ready, set, go!"

The Brabenders started to shovel the gelatinous fish into their mouths at high speed. Almost instantaneously, Reggie threw up into the large, potted plant next to their table. It had been a month since their last lutefisk supper, so he could barely smell Vince's puke from last time.

"Whoa!" Brett said. "Reggie, that was some impressive projectile!" He turned to Vince. "How does it feel to be knocked off by *your* little brother?"

"Shut up!" Vince yelled.

"Suck it!" Curly squealed.

Reggie raised his arms in triumph and proclaimed, "Vomit King!" Never in his life had Reggie been so excited to accidentally eat a hair, but it was that hair, probably from Mrs. Larson, that had induced the instant puke fest into the potted plants. Bart and his wife never understood why their kids always raced to the corner table by the plants, but it was a matter of practicality for the Brabender boys.

Across the room, Mrs. Helstrom, wearing her colorful *bunad* and silver *sølje* jewelry, stood at the dessert table unwrapping packages of *lefse*. She was late in setting up because she had to clean up the root beer that Gunnar Smith had knocked over when he was playing catch indoors with Brett Brabender. *Unbelievable! Throwing the ball indoors!* she'd silently screamed in her head. Of course, neither Mrs. Smith nor Mrs. Brabender were around to discipline their awful children. Gunnar uncharacteristically offered to help clean, but he spent the whole time making it worse by spreading it around and spilling more. Then he suddenly got up and went to sit with Brett. Mrs. Helstrom decided she was going to talk with their mothers as soon as she got home.

As she picked up a new package of *lefse*, she noticed a note with a photograph taped to it. She immediately recognized the musky mailbox in the photo as hers. The name *Helstrom* was clearly painted across the side in her handwriting. There was another mailbox in the photo, too. She held it an arm's length to see better, because she was *not* getting her reading glasses that made her look old. The photo finally came into focus, and she gasped when she realized that she was looking at Mr. Postie in a sexually compromising position with another musky mailbox that was holding a Canadian flag. The message on the note, written with letters clipped from magazines, said, "O, Canada! O, Canada! O, CANADA! I swam north to visit my Canadian lover."

If there was one thing that Mrs. Helstrom hated as much as perverse sexual imagery, it was Canadians. She had a particular disdain for the neighbors to the north. She viewed them as a population that could have been American but just didn't have the resolve to fully commit to the principles of capitalism, evangelicalism, and consumerism. Plus, she certainly didn't trust a country whose money looked like something out of a child's board game, even if the ludicrous one-dollar coin (a coin!) had a picture of a loon.

"Who did this?" she yelled, holding the note in the air. "Who did this?"

Brett winked at Gunnar, who at the moment was trying not to gag on his third spoonful of lutefisk.

Taylor Helstrom, who was filling her plate with cookies, giggled when she saw the photo that her mom was waving around. Mrs. Helstrom did not think that was funny—at all—so she took her daughter's plate of cookies.

"Oh, no one did this? I don't think so!" She stared down the room of puzzled Lutherans, who were too polite to ask her why she was flipping out. When no one came forward, she began to box up all the dessert. "OK, you ruined it for everyone. I hope you're happy!"

Brett and Gunnar definitely were happy. They grabbed dessert before they spilled the soda because they knew what happened when one unleashed the fury of Mrs. Helstrom.

Later that evening, the Lake News 37 television news anchors, Michael Gunderson and Melanie Chevalier, updated Mistakers on the horrible thefts.

"Tonight on Lake News 37," began Melanie, very seriously, "deadly, melting icicles hang off Mistake City Hall. Only Lake News 37 has the exclusive street corners to avoid."

"Oh, brother, it's May, for Pete's sake!" Michael chimed in. He had been hired for being excellent at lightening the mood, and was the go-to "on a lighter note" guy in northern Wisconsin.

"Are freezing temperatures still possible? We'll let you know what this means for your garden, and whether you need to get out the bedsheet tonight."

"Sheesh, Mother Nature! It's May, you know!" Michael was really good at his job.

Melanie prepared her deepest voice. It was the one that she used when she was hoping to win a local broadcasting award. "But first on Lake News 37, the Musky Mailbox Mystery."

Immediately, the "Musky Mailbox Mystery" graphics package went full frame on the screen, with the musky mailboxes popping up, then fading away as a huge magnifying glass swooped over them. Crime scene tape with the words *Musky Mailbox Mystery* darted in from the left with a crashing sting. The tape fell to the bottom of the screen as Melanie began reading the chilling details and throwing to press conference sound bites.

The graphics team was thrilled with how slick everything looked. They had gone through four ideas for naming the story, settling on the fifth, "Musky Mailbox Mystery." The first four were deemed too punny for Lake News 37 viewers to understand: "The Postman Rings Never Because Your Mailbox Is Gone," "Wait a Minute, Mr. Postman," "Return to Sender," and "War on Musky Mailbox Terror." They might have gone with the fourth option, but the news director didn't like how the graphics team just reused the Iraq-Afghanistan package with a mailbox pasted over the Saddam Hussein statue. Simple, the director insisted, was best to convey the urgency of the message.

"If you have any information on these dangerous thieves, please report all tips to Sheriff Holm. You can find her information on our Lake News 37 website." Melanie knew how important it was for viewers to get all information directly linked from the Lake News 37 site instead of telling viewers the actual websites with the information. More advertising-revenue click-throughs meant more free golf for her at the Lake Mistake Country Club, and she needed to keep up appearances to show her ex-husband what he was missing.

"And now, on a lighter note, let's see what Bob and Bonnie are up to." Michael always introduced the "Fishin' with Bob 'n' Bonnie" segments. Bob and Bonnie were a married couple in their forties who provided the Lake News 37 viewers with valuable fishing advice and a boatload of adorableness. They were beloved celebrities in Mistake, and locals always bought Bob and Bonnie drinks to thank them for that one tip that landed them a monster fish. The last time that Bob and Bonnie paid for a brandy old-fashioned was more than a decade ago, when they were at a wedding below the bridge on Michigan's Lower Peninsula where no one knew who they were.

Bonnie was also a huge hit with teenagers ever since her fishing fail became the most viewed online video in Lake News 37 history. What kid didn't want to see an old lady pulled over the side of a boat by a huge musky and then dragged around Lake Stockholm by the five-foot beast?

Today, Bob and Bonnie were standing in their fishing boat, still in the trailer and parked in their driveway. With most of the lakes still iced over and whatnot, they'd decided they would demonstrate their musky fishing tips on dry land. As Bonnie discussed Opening Day weather, Bob accidentally hooked his musky mailbox while casting his spinner bait. He ripped off the fin flag, which hit Bonnie in the face.

"Oh, that Bob!" Michael said with a chuckle. "What a card!"

ELEVEN

Downstairs, Cheryl Svenson sat glued to the TV reports about the Musky Mailbox Task Force. Upstairs, Megan couldn't care less. Nor could her best friend, Kaitlyn Smith.

Megan and Kaitlyn were supposed to be working on a project for English class that they had been putting off because, like all normal people, they had zero interest in comparing poets of the Romantic era. Despite meeting specifically to work on their report, they were working on much more important things that evening, like planning what they were going to wear to Bridget Frigaard's Opening Day boathouse party. It was a delicate balance of combining swimsuits, jeans, and the newest fishing shirts from Nielsen's.

After taking care of the critical sartorial decisions, Megan and Kaitlyn realized how late it was getting and finally sat down at the computer. They couldn't believe they'd been so sidetracked that they almost missed the online debut of country singer Ben Kvam's new music video. Kvam was the most popular country star in Wisconsin, Minnesota, and North Dakota. He was a favorite of students at Mistake High because he grew up eighty miles west in the village of Ottawaumegon.

"(Always) Set the Hook," Kvam's hit fishing-inspired party anthem, was last fall's official homecoming song. It was the perfect tune for Mattie the Musky to use for revving up the football crowd to fish for their fourth conference championship (which didn't happen). As per homecoming tradition, all students attending the game wore fishing hats, fishing shirts, and fishing vests decorated with colorful lures. Some of the more creative girls turned bobbers into earrings, six pairs of which needed to be removed by wire cutters after several freshmen forgot to swap out the fishhooks for earring hooks.

In addition to the jewelry mishap, there were plenty of other fishhooks flying around the stands that night because students had also brought fishing poles and nets to the game. Brett had been on JV that fall, so he was in the stands with Gunnar and the rest of their teammates. They didn't pay much attention to the game because they were 100 percent focused on trying to hook the skirt of any cheerleader with their fishing lines. After several attempts at casting in the direction of the cutest girls on the squad, a rogue gust of wind carried Gunnar's line into Mrs. Helstrom's Mattie the Musky hat. The result was equal parts thrilling and terrifying.

Mrs. Helstrom was sitting in the usual section that she loudly claimed for Mistake Lutheran (ELCA) members. She didn't notice the hook in her hat because she was too distracted by keeping rival Lutheran synod members away from the staked-out ELCA seats. Mrs. Helstrom was well-known for having absolutely zero sense of humor, which is why Mistake's teenagers called her the Hell Storm. Usually, her outbursts were funny, but sometimes they were more trouble than they were worth. So after a huge high five, Brett advised Gunnar to cut the line because their evening would be ruined if he began reeling in. Brett reached into the breast pocket on his fishing vest and pulled out a pair of nail clippers.

"So long, Moby Dick," said Gunnar, using a reference that he recently learned in English class. It was also a classy way to slide the word *dick* into conversation. Both Gunnar and Brett snickered.

When leaving the game that night, some poor freshman inadvertently stepped on the long fishing line attached to the hook and pulled the hat off Mrs. Helstrom's head. The Hell Storm descended upon him and his girlfriend until Pastor Jennifer of Mistake Lutheran (ELCA) stepped in and assured Mrs. Helstrom that there was no conspiracy to get her hat dirty and mess up her hair.

Things started looking up for the boys when Brett made the catch of the day by hooking the skirt of his main target, sophomore cheerleader Bridget Frigaard. Just like in the song, he set the hook and up went Bridget's skirt. She was furious, but mainly because a JV player and not a varsity player had hooked her. Brett was so busy celebrating with his friends that he didn't notice Bridget ripping out the hook and wrapping the line around her hand. She yanked the line as hard as she could and pulled Brett headfirst into the large fishing net Lina Svenson was holding in the row in front of him. It was the greatest moment of Lina's life, which she immediately documented with a selfie and promptly uploaded to every social media website to which she belonged.

As Lina photographed Brett, Bridget casually unwrapped the fishing line from her hand, threw it on the ground, and continued dancing to "Do The Musky" along with the rest of the cheerleading squad. "Do The Musky" was a 1990s hit novelty song and dance in Wisconsin that was inspired by the Musky Slide and was recorded and released by the Crappie Boys, a local wedding band. The ridiculous dance was as popular at weddings as the chicken dance and the polka.

But not even "Do The Musky" could match the excitement of watching a new music video from Ben Kvam that Sunday night in Megan's bedroom. "Turn it up! I can't hear!" Kaitlyn reached over Megan's shoulder to punch the volume key on the computer. She looked toward the window. "What's all that noise outside?"

"The gun club. They just switched to extended summer hours."

"Obviously. I mean, who's outside talking?" Kaitlyn said, referring to the voices beneath Megan's window. It was definitely too late for anyone's parents to be outside because the ten p.m. news had already started.

Megan got up to look out the window. "It's just Brett and your stupid brother messing around in the boat."

"What a liar! Gunnar told me that he was at Steve Rogberg's working on this stupid poetry thing too!" Kaitlyn said without taking her eyes off the music video.

Megan opened the window and pressed her face up to the screen. "Hey, dummies!"

Upon hearing a voice, Gunnar and Brett hastily adjusted a blanket that covered the mailboxes they'd just finished moving into the boat from the truck.

"What are you doing?" Megan called.

"What are *you* doing? Mind your own business!" Brett yelled as he dove in front of an exposed musky mailbox tail and pushed it back under the blanket.

"Hi, Megan!" Gunnar said, waving. *It's just like Juliet in the balcony scene,* he thought.

Megan rolled her eyes. Kaitlyn managed to tear herself away from the computer and popped up in the open window to yell to her twin brother. "Aren't you supposed to be doing English, Gunnar?"

"Already done."

"Yeah, right," Kaitlyn said. She was right, of course. Gunnar knew that Steve would be able to copy an essay from one of the many girls that had a crush on him. Such was the power of a school soccer star who'd also bagged the biggest buck last Thanksgiving.

Suddenly, lights illuminated the front yard as a WCSD car drove past the house, presumably a Musky Mailbox Task Force deputy hot on the case.

"Hey, man," Brett said to Gunnar. "We gotta move the boat into the garage."

Gunnar was too busy being lost in thought as he stared at Megan to notice Brett's question.

"Brett, when are you taking Gunnar home? Can I get a ride?" Kaitlyn asked. "I don't want to have to call my mom."

"Yeah, whatever," Brett said as he threw a handful of fake worms at Gunnar's face to get his attention away from Megan. "Dude! We have to get the boat into the garage. Now."

"Oh, right, yeah. The garage." Gunnar hopped out of the boat with Brett, and they began pushing it into the garage.

"What do you have in there?" Megan asked, pointing. The boat was so full, there was nowhere to sit.

"New fishing gear. For Opening Day," Brett answered.

"That's all fishing gear?" Megan challenged.

"What, you work in a bait shop for six months, and you know everything about fishing?" From the garage, Brett checked to make sure that the blankets still covered the mailboxes.

"Well, I know you need to be able to move around the boat."

"Shut up."

"I'm getting my things and coming down. We're going home now, Gunnar," Kaitlyn said.

"Bye, Megan!" Gunnar turned around to wave, but the window was already shut.

Brett punched a code into the garage-door keypad to close the door safely.

TWELVE

That Sunday evening, while the citizens of Mistake organized their neighborhood watches and the Musky Mailbox Task Force began patrols, three oblivious Whole Lotta Bait businessmen decided to party. The top guys from Whole Lotta Bait's marketing department, Dan Schweitzman, Harold Leclerc, and Axl McCool, were in Mistake to scope out the bait market and obtain the building permit from the Troll.

They had arrived in Mistake two days earlier, after a drive from Chicago that left them too tired to explore the area. So they'd picked up a case of beer at the gas station and spent the evening looking for evidence of the gangster history of Shady Pines Lodge on Lake Stockholm. After drinking several beers, they were pretty sure that they'd discovered two bullet holes in the kitchen that they hadn't seen earlier in the day. They had specifically requested Cabin #8 Lil' Moose because it had been the home base of the famed Chicago gangster Walt Balistrioto, aka the Birdwatcher, aka Waltie Balls.

Back in the 1920s, Mistake was prime real estate for Chicago syndicate mobsters who wanted peace, quiet, and cops who were willing to take a bribe. The gangsters were based in the Northwoods to wait for illegal booze that was flown in from Canada. They boxed up the hooch and sent it down to Chicago, where it was distributed to the finest speakeasies. Waltie Balls worked out of Lil' Moose as he watched the skies for Monday and Thursday arrivals of Canadian whiskey and gin. Each time the seaplane landed on the lake, he waved his flag to direct the plane over to his cabin, where work could begin. The owner of Shady Pines Lodge was more than happy to have his land serve as the Birdwatcher's hideout because of the never-ending supply of whiskey and women. On his off-days, Waltie Balls focused his attention on the whorehouse that he had established on Main Street. Madame Agnes's brothel was now the location of a popular Italian restaurant, Balistrioto's.

After a solid night of sleep, Schweitzman, Leclerc, and McCool woke up early to start fishing for the famous Mistake muskies. But when they got to Brabender's Bait, the dumb girl behind the counter didn't seem to understand opening day despite people obviously fishing on the lakes. They didn't really care about the fine print, though. In fact, they never cared about the fine print. If they got fined, they just planned on adding it to their business-trip expenses. Luckily for them, the WCSD was too busy with the Musky Mailbox Task Force to patrol waters for tourists in violation of musky fishing season.

Even though it was almost summer, there was plenty of late-season ice on the water. Some lakes were still frozen—a bummer for the guys since they didn't know how to ice fish. When they finally got Schweitzman's boat onto Lake Stockholm, they didn't even catch any muskies. They mostly caught largemouth bass and bluegill that they quickly tossed back into the water.

They were convinced that the girl at the bait shop had given them lazy suckers and minnows. Whole Lotta Bait minnows were going to blow the ones sold at Brabender's out of the water. Whole Lotta Bait minnows lived in specially aerated tanks that pumped fresh oxygen into the water at an incredibly high rate. This pushed the fish around so much that they looked like the liveliest bait customers had ever seen—which meant they bought twice as much.

McCool had already updated the Kaczmarski cousins about the local fishing scene, the bait-shop competition, and their success at obtaining the permit from the Troll. The Whole Lotta Bait crew assumed they could just conduct business with the Troll at Shady Pines Lodge, but the Troll thought the exchange needed to be more cloak-and-dagger.

McCool followed the Troll's meticulous instructions to the letter that Sunday afternoon, including driving to the hidden, swampy side of the Nimrod Lodge on Waushauna Lake and waiting for the Troll to blow on his duck call. The problem was that the Whole Lotta Bait guys had no idea what a duck call sounded like, so they never lit the cigarette in response. They had even purchased cigarettes for the occasion, and they didn't smoke. Cigarettes, that is. They certainly smoked cigars, like any self-respecting businessmen.

After the Troll blew the duck call three times in vain, he stepped out of the shadows on the other side of a tiny inlet. These were obviously the right men judging from the way they discussed the new draft picks for the Chicago Bears. The Troll angrily whispered, "Hey!"

The bros were taken aback by the man in camouflage and face paint, but they eventually realized that the man with the wooden kazoo must be the Troll with their permit.

"The duck chases the fish into the water," the Troll whispered loudly.

"What?" asked McCool, looking around for ducks.

The Troll tossed the permit over to the guys. It was sealed inside a plastic mayonnaise jar. Puzzled, McCool watched as the jar flew through the air and landed in the slushy water near the shore (the Troll was never known for his aim).

Leclerc fished the wet jar out of the cold water and examined it. "It's the permit," he said.

McCool was starting to wonder whether the Troll actually lived under a bridge.

"Thanks, man," Leclerc said. "We'll be in touch."

The three men turned to walk back to their SUV when the Troll interrupted.

"Wait!" He paused to look around for any spies. "Where's my...you know."

McCool turned back to the Troll. "You'll get it when this checks out. Meet us back here on Wednesday morning."

A Wisconsin state representative had already cooked up the special boathouse permit for the Troll. This particular representative, a good friend of the Kaczmarski family, had successfully dismissed four corruption charges in the past year alone. He wasn't worried about losing his job because he represented one of the most gerrymandered districts in the nation. His district lines were so ridiculously drawn that his constituency was known as the dick district, both because it looked like one on a political map and because of the misogynistic views of its inhabitants. Unless he did something stupid, like demand that women should be paid as much as men, he was guaranteed reelection in the fall no matter what he did.

Now, after the successful acquisition of the building permit, it was finally time to celebrate. Schweitzman was getting remarried next month, so McCool and Leclerc threw him a mini bachelor party with the finest guy activities that Mistake could offer. After a delicious Italian dinner at Balistrioto's, served by a waitress so hot that they made a note to hire her to be the first Mistake Whole Lotta Girl, they rented some rifles from a dude next to Brabender's and drove out to the woods to snipe some trees. After a general assault on the sugar maples, they tried to snipe their names into the bark, but their aim was nonexistent. Instead, they took out two opossums, one squirrel, and a lot of leaves.

A few more beers and a couple rounds later, the men stood silent as they tried to figure out what else they could do at two a.m. on a Monday in Mistake when all of the bars were closed.

"Now what?" McCool slurred.

"Look, I can see my breath," Leclerc said.

"Maybe we should go deer hunting," Schweitzman suggested.

"Do you think Capone buried treasure up here?"

"Man, how cool would it be to be a baller like Capone," Leclerc said with a longing sigh. He wanted to spray the empty field with more bullets to demonstrate his best St. Valentine's Day Massacre reenactment, but he was out of ammunition.

It was at this moment that inspiration struck Schweitzman. "Wait, I have the brochure!"

"The what?" McCool said and burped.

"From the cabin." Schweitzman pulled it out of his back pocket, opened it, and studied it carefully, even though it was impossible to read in the dark. He pulled out his phone and used the screen's light to find what he was looking for. "Aha!" He pointed toward Waushauna Lake down the road.

The bros had the most awesome time skidding across the melting ice in their car. It was barely thick enough to hold their SUV, but it did. Until they decided that it would be even more awesome to snipe the ice.

THIRTEEN

The classrooms of Mistake High School should have been filled with gossip about the countdown to Friday's Opening Day festivities, such as who was fishing with whom, who was bringing beer to the pontoon party, and plenty of smack talk about who was going to catch the biggest musky. The excitement should have been palpable, much like the week before deer hunting in November when no one could concentrate on anything other than praying for snow to make tracking easier.

Instead, anger seethed through the hallways that Monday morning. Opening Day, glorious day-off-from-school Opening Day, had been canceled. By the Troll. Officially, the Troll canceled Opening Day as punishment until the musky mailbox thieves were found. Unofficially, the Troll canceled Opening Day to maintain the media frenzy that distracted everyone from his Whole Lotta Bait activities.

Teachers were as annoyed as the students. They didn't want to come into school on Friday, either. Whatever. They'd spend all day showing movies. As far as the students were concerned, the freaking Troll's reign of terror on the teenagers of Mistake continued, ruining everything they held dear. Megan wasn't surprised. She figured the Troll would do something despicable. But canceling Opening Day? The reign of terror had finally gone too far.

It all started in September, when the Troll successfully passed a bill in city council to build an enclosed luxury box at the high school football stadium. This might not have pissed off the student body if they had been given access to the box, but the only people allowed to sit in there were local government officials. Construction of the box coincided with a price increase in student football tickets from one dollar to five dollars. Protests were staged and homes were egged, but the Troll remained steadfast in his belief that students should foot the bill. No one else on the city council objected because they were too busy enjoying the heated space and beer service to their new cushioned seats at football games.

The second incident in the reign of terror occurred at the start of spring semester when students returned from Christmas break. Their favorite cafeteria Tater Tots had been replaced with head cheese, a gross, meat-jelly, cold-cut "food" made from pieces of flesh from a pig's head! Aside from being forced to sample the disgusting meat during fourth grade when studying Wisconsin pioneer life, very few teenagers in their right minds willingly ate head cheese unless a class grade depended on it. The students tried a hunger strike, which quickly fell apart when the scent of fried bacon wafted over from the cafeteria kitchen. As soon as the senior-class vice president found out that the Troll ordered the menu change, students stole all of the head cheese and threw it at the deputy mayor's house. It became known as The Head Cheesing. But the Troll didn't care. Not only did he like head cheese, the kickback from the local pig farmers was massive and going toward his boathouse.

The cancellation of Opening Day was the final straw with the students. No one knew what to do, but action was required. Megan was on a warpath. She hated the Troll for what she saw as targeted attacks on everyone at Mistake High, all for his personal gain. She didn't know what his angle was this time, but she was going to get to the bottom of it—or at least annoy him.

Like she'd done after the other incidents, Megan turned to her online blog for the high school paper. Luckily, first period for Megan was study hall, so she had plenty of time to write about Opening Day and post a special edition of *Uff Da*. By the end of second period, Megan was on the receiving end of numerous high fives in the hall. By the end of third period, the Troll was on the phone with Principal Pam Jansen, demanding the un-American post be removed immediately. Unfortunately for the Troll, Principal Jansen had been signed up to compete in the now-canceled fishing contest.

"You can't publish this!" the Troll screamed into his phone. "It's one hundred percent slanderous!"

"I think you mean libelous. And it's not."

"Remove this from the website at once! By the order of the mayor!"

"Perhaps if you hadn't canceled the most important day of the year, this article wouldn't exist," Principal Jansen said calmly. Then she hung up.

Infuriated by the principal's inaction, the Troll seethed as he reread the offending words that glowed from his computer screen:

"Opening Day?! Opening Day?!? The Troll officially hates Mistake's teenagers. While the mailbox thefts are wrong, does he need to punish all teens and the community? There isn't any proof that one of us did it. But it does represent one more targeted mistreatment of students at Mistake High School for no reason.

"Or is there? What does the Troll have against us? We never did anything to him. Heck, some of us even voted him into office. And yet he continues to target us. First, by a 500 percent increase on football tickets so that he can sit with his cronies in a box, and then the disgusting head-cheese scheme. (BRING BACK OUR TOTS!) His unchecked power needs to be checked. The Troll must be stopped before his next move. He's abusing his power, either as a megalomaniac or to hide something.

"This time, he claims he's trying to punish the mailbox thieves. Well, why does he assume it's someone from Mistake? Sheriff Holm has no evidence to support his theories. Is he protecting his teens from his hometown of

Waunomonee, our school rival? What are you hiding, Troll?"

The Troll slammed his laptop closed and tried to think of someone to hack into the school website. Unfortunately, everyone he knew who could hack a website was a student at Mistake High School. In search of happier news, he checked his phone for an update on his permit from the Whole Lotta Bait guys. Nothing.

FOURTEEN

Velkommen! That was the cheerful greeting on the red sign, painted in Norwegian rosemaling that hung behind the large bar in the Nimrod Lodge. In true Northwoods juxtaposition, the welcome sign hung above an old tommy gun that had been fished out of Waushauna Lake back in 1984. Both were displayed between a twenty-three-point buck and a seventeen-point buck, both shot decades ago by founder Bill Eckerstorfer.

The tavern room at the lodge was where the prized macho trophies of Mistake were displayed because it meant that everyone would see them. It was like the community family room. Why hang an elk at home when more people can admire it at the lodge? There was the legendary bear that local mom Susie Galineau killed when she saw it destroying her petunias; a wolf that John Petersson, the founder of the Chitchat Supper Club, had trapped; a fifty-pound musky that an eighteen-year-old had caught during the bicentennial; and three chipmunks a young Mike Zwicky shot during the 1974 chipmunk infestation. There were also a handful of high school football trophies on display near the window.

But the prize trophy, positively screaming with Americana, hung over the fireplace: a stuffed bald eagle from the good old days, shot by the first Mistake postmaster when hunting the birds was legal.

Day and night, old men sat around the bar, drank, and told tall tales about the glory days before the Internet ruined the world. These guys were the only Nimrods who regularly wore the Order of the Nimrods lapel pin, which depicted a shotgun and a musky that crossed to make an X. Younger men and families would filter in during the afternoon and evening. Many kids got their first taste of beer at the Nimrod Lodge since it was legal in Wisconsin for children to be served alcohol as long as their parents were present. Kids didn't care about the origin of the unique law, but it was generally attributed to the beer-drinking traditions of German immigrants. It certainly made for some lively wedding receptions in the tavern room, like the time all of the Brabender boys got in a Packers versus Vikings fistfight with their Minnesota cousins. Luckily, the Brabenders morphed into "I love you, man" drunks as the night wore on, and by the end of the evening, they were all arm in arm and singing "America the Beautiful" under the stuffed eagle.

During the summer, most lodge action was by the boat pier on Waushauna Lake and the large fish-cleaning shed. That smelly shack was constantly full of people, flies, and grateful raccoons at all hours from May to September. During the colder months, the lodge was a required stop on all snowmobile trips, so that riders could refuel with a hot toddy before heading back into the elements. Some cities in the Northwoods championed silent winter sports, like snowshoeing or cross-country skiing, but Mistake fully supported the rights of all Americans to loudly race gas-guzzling machines over frozen lakes, dodging the ice-shanties like obstacles in a video game.

Back in the early days, admittance to the Order of Nimrods meant that applicants had to have bagged a buck or a musky over a certain weight. The rules were more relaxed now, and Mistakers could become Nimrods based on legacy status if their hunting was sub-par. That was how Bill Eckerstorfer's great-great-grandson became the current leader, and he made sure his best friend rose through the ranks with him. Both Grand Leader Eckerstorfer, Esteemed Nimrod, and his second in command, Brother Superior Bjorling, Esteemed Nimrod, were in their fifties and had been running the lodge for the past decade.

The lodge's absolute busiest time was the nine days surrounding Thanksgiving—deer-hunting season! The most wonderful time of the year! The hunting widows and kids hung out at the lodge, aka *deer camp*, waiting to see what Dad or Mom brought back. After a successful kill, hunters usually field dressed the deer in the woods (more grateful raccoons!), then dragged the carcass to the Nimrod Lodge. The lodge was a DNR registration station where hunters registered their kill with officials, and Grand Leader Eckerstorfer handed out "My First Deer" badges to junior hunters. After registration, hunters grabbed a beer and swapped butchering tips with their buddies as they waited to see who bagged the biggest buck. Nimrods with the most impressive deer were allowed to hang the carcass inside the converted fish-cleaning shed. Sometimes there were so many successful hunters that the lodge had to bring in basketball hoops because they ran out of meat hooks for hanging the deer. The high school polka band provided music for the entire nine-day event, except for a brief break for Thanksgiving dinner and any Packers games.

After spending the day fielding angry calls about the cancellation of Opening Day, Sheriff Holm escaped her office to head to the Nimrod Lodge. She knew that conducting official interviews on behalf of the Musky Mailbox Task Force was a pointless exercise because she had already interviewed the victims, like Mrs. Helstrom, at the time of the crime. She hated the wasted repeat effort, especially when she drove past the lakes full of unlicensed tourists. But she had a part to play in Mayor Ole's task-force circus, and the lodge was a good cross-section of Mistakers that would provide the various points of view required for the status updates to the mayor.

She figured that the mailboxes were stashed safely somewhere in town, and they would miraculously reappear piled in the middle of the woods or something when the kids started to feel guilty. Sinking the boxes in a lake to hide the evidence would be too much effort, since many lakes were still covered in a dangerous, slushy mess of ice. Plus, nothing could be returned if it were at the bottom of a lake, resulting in even more guilt as the boxes rotted away in the weeds. If they had been stolen by teenagers hell-bent on destruction, there would have already been smashed musky mailbox parts littered around Mistake. The photo that Mrs. Helstrom e-mailed to her last night (Subject: *URGENT MMTF hooliganism evidence!!*) proved her theory that some kids were just goofing off. Sheriff Holm was usually on the money in matters concerning Mistake's teenage population.

Deputy Holm became Sheriff Holm when she was elected two years ago in a landslide. It was the best turnout for eighteen- to twenty-year-old voters ever recorded in a Waumabenon County election. Her popularity with that age group was a direct result of her leniency with underage drinking. As long as she didn't catch them doing meth or heroin, she couldn't be bothered with busting drinking parties in the woods. The paperwork and angry calls from parents just weren't worth the time or effort. If she came across wasted teens, she just made them promise not to drive any cars, snowmobiles, or boats.

But she couldn't ignore the Musky Mailbox Task Force, not with all the media coverage drummed up with that idiotic press conference yesterday. The coverage included Megan's blog post, which led to the Troll leaving frantic voice mails demanding that she shut down the school's website. Megan was also sending messages to her about possible theories of the Troll's involvement in the crime. Sheriff Holm's phone beeped all night, so she barely slept.

After pulling up to the Nimrod, she had little patience for the usual barrage from the old geezers smoking outside.

As she walked up the steps, Old Geezer One gestured to Sheriff Holm with his cigarette and said to his buddy, "Remember back when women weren't even allowed in?"

"We used to have a darts room. Now it's a powder room," sneered Old Geezer Two as he took a drag on his cigarette.

"What a shame," agreed Old Geezer One before launching into a smoke-induced coughing fit.

"No more darts."

Sheriff Holm paused as she opened the lodge door. "You ever play darts?"

Old Geezer Two looked at her incredulously. "What am I? A darn limey?"

"Pool!" Old Geezer One wheezed, finding it difficult to inhale a new puff of smoke with the lingering coughs. "That's what Americans play!"

"You betcha!" Old Geezer Two agreed. Both of them stared at her, smoking, coughing, and judging her overall crime of being a woman.

Sheriff Holm tried not to look like she had noticed Old Geezer One's open fly. A few months ago, after the third occasion of mentioning it to him and receiving a lewd remark in reply, she realized that he usually left his fly open on purpose.

"OK, then, you gentlemen enjoy your day," she said. She opened the door and stepped into a mass of red helium balloons. The lodge was being decorated for its annual *Syttende Mai* dance, held in honor of Norway's Constitution Day, so it was bursting with red-and-white balloons and Norwegian flags. While admiring the handiwork of whoever had wrapped red-and-white crepe paper around the massive antlers of the stuffed buck, she immediately came under fire from Grand Leader Eckerstorfer, Esteemed Nimrod.

"How come you haven't caught anyone?"

It was difficult for Sheriff Holm not to take this as a personal attack. During her campaign for sheriff, Eckerstorfer had very publicly supported the strong, resolute, male candidate because Waumabenon didn't need a lady sheriff with lady problems.

"Come on, now. You know I can't discuss that."

"The mayor said this was his number-one priority, so I've been organizing the neighborhood watch," said Eckerstorfer with his judgment-filled face. "I'm not going to let them get away with it again."

Ugh. I hope I catch your kids red-handed. Sheriff Holm fantasized about parading his handcuffed children in front of him. Like most parents of bratty kids, Eckerstorfer was blind to the fact that his precious offspring were always on the list of usual suspects for any occurrence of vandalism.

"I'm on first shift over in Pinewood," said Wayne Krumpelmann, who was standing on a ladder and hanging Norwegian flags. Pinewood was the new part of town and filled with McMansions. It was a place where the neighborhood association required that all lawns be mowed in a diagonal pattern. The Troll was a Pinewood resident, which meant that the streets of that neighborhood were always immediately plowed following any trace of snow, even though the road salt and plows were based in the old part of town. Five mailboxes had gone missing in Pinewood, and the neighborhood was on high alert regarding this major catastrophe.

"My shotgun and I will be on the porch from sunset till midnight," Krumpelmann said.

"I don't think a shotgun is necessary, Mr. Krumpelmann. I'd prefer that you leave it locked in your house, in fact."

"But sheriff, the mayor said we need to stop these terrorists by all means necessary. So did the Troll."

"Especially if it's those blasted chipmunks," said an old drunk at the bar. He picked up an imaginary gun and shot the imaginary chipmunks. "Pow, pow, *pow!*"

"Chipmunks didn't steal two dozen mailboxes."

"Well, no one thought they would commandeer the Nimrod float and drive it into the sweet-corn stand back in the '74 parade, but they did!" Old Drunk looked pleased with himself for his superior argument.

"That didn't happen, either. Look, guys, it's just kids being stupid." Sheriff Holm took out her notebook so that she had a stronger air of authority. People tended to be more thoughtful with their words when they knew they were being recorded. "Anyone come in here talking about weird stuff they've seen? You know, something that didn't seem quite right in the neighborhood? Maybe a large tarp covering something that wasn't there before, or a minivan with more stuff than usual in the back?"

"Chipmunks attacked my dog," Old Drunk persisted.

"Anything besides chipmunks?"

"The Burdettes got TP'd last night," Krumpelmann offered. "You hear about that, Grand Leader? Pretty impressive use of the old two-ply."

"There were more drawings in Loon Hollow, the chalk ones," Eckerstorfer said with disappointment, as if this were Sheriff Holm's fault.

Krumpelmann stroked his beard as he thought. "You know, come to think of it, I saw some weird Chicago fellows out back. Those city slickers don't normally come near the lodge."

"So these guys from Chicago," the sheriff said in her best I'm-taking-you-seriously-even-though-I-don't voice. "They drove all the way up here to steal mailboxes, you're thinking?"

"Well, I don't know why they'd want them. But they were just kind of weird out there."

"In what way?"

"They were talking to the Troll. And he was dressed like he was going duck hunting."

Eckerstorfer turned to Sheriff Holm to translate for the female-impaired. "It's not duck season."

Sheriff Holm ignored him and continued talking to Krumpelmann. "Oh yeah? Did you hear what they were saying?"

"No, but those Chicago guys got real excited when the Troll threw a mayo jar at them. Yeah, that was kinda weird, too."

FIFTEEN

It was a lovely Tuesday morning, one of the warmest of the year. The birds were finally singing! Mrs. Helstrom hummed a song as she opened the door to get the morning paper and saw something taped to Sunny, her front-porch garden gnome. She bent down, and a look of horror and disgust washed over her face when she saw that it was another photo of her dear musky mailbox. This time, Mr. Postie was in a compromising position with a teddy bear that had Chicago Bears pants around his ankles.

She looked around angrily and unsuccessfully tried to yell a complete thought. "Mr. Postie! How can—You won't—I'm—Your mother—Perverts! Argh!"

With that, Mrs. Helstrom went inside to call Sheriff Holm to report more MMTF hooliganism evidence.

"Oh, man, did you see her face?" Gunnar giggled as he and Brett walked through school.

"She was all like, 'My precious Mr. Postie!'" shrieked Brett in his best Mrs. Helstrom voice. "Classic Hell Storm!"

Mrs. Helstrom had been in Brett's sights since she'd called the cops on him last month for toilet-papering the Frigaards' house next door. Being Mrs. Helstrom, someone on constant high alert for any wrongdoing, she totally failed to understand that it was because Brett had a crush on Bridget Frigaard. Hell Storm had been so concerned about the possibility of toilet paper blowing into her yard that she obviously didn't notice the "Spring dance?" written on the driveway in shaving cream. Neither did Bridget. Though, to be fair, the shaving cream invitation didn't last long enough for her to see it. As soon as Brett left the Frigaards, several raccoons had pawed at the foam, thinking it might be part of a tasty late-night snack. Overall, the whole thing had cost Brett fifty dollars at the drugstore, which he had taken from his mom's wallet, and the time it took to scribble an apology card that his mom had made him write.

As payback, he stole Mrs. Helstrom's beloved musky mailbox just to see her reaction. When he told Gunnar about the Hell Storm's scene in the Svensons' driveway, they decided to steal more to see how many they could collect. They didn't really have any idea what they were going to do with them, other than send notes to Mrs. Helstrom documenting the sexual adventures of Mr. Postie.

Now Brett was in desperate need of a new place to hide the mailboxes, because his dad was going to use the boat for musky fishing on Friday, regardless of Opening Day festivities being canceled. He knew that he couldn't just secretly take them to the city dump after former classmate

Chad Bjorling had been caught last year dumping a bunch of plastic baby Jesuses that he'd stolen from church nativities. Chad didn't see what the big deal was. He had replaced them in the mangers with Mattie the Musky plush toys that were wearing his Mistake High class's color of blaze orange because *seniors rule!* Chad hadn't done his research on the city dump, because the research didn't involve boobs, so he didn't know that he had to declare his trash when entering the landfill site.

Brett turned to Gunnar and lowered his voice. "Did you find any space in your mom's gardening shed?"

"Nah, man. My mom's been in and out of that place all week. She's all, 'I'm so late on tomato planting!' or something. Isn't there room in your garage?"

"I thought there was space behind the snowmobiles, but that's where Dad stashed the extra cases of plastic worms for the store."

"Bummer."

Brett did have one last-ditch idea, though. It all depended on the crush he knew that a certain freshman had on him. A freshman that he knew would be standing behind him, because she was always behind him.

"Hey, Lina," Brett said, without turning around.

"Yes, Brett!"

Brett rolled his eyes as he smiled at Gunnar. *Of course she's there*, thought Brett. "You think you can do a favor for me?"

"Oh my gosh, yes!"

Brett turned around and smiled at her. "S'up, Lina? Looking good today."

"Whatever you want."

"I need to borrow some space in your basement."

"Oh, sure!"

"And you'll help me move my stuff down there?"

"Yeah!"

"And you won't tell Megan about it?"

"Oh my god, no! Never!"

"Cool. Thanks, Lina." He gave her a little jock nod and continued walking down the hallway after a quick fist bump with Gunnar.

"You're welcome, Brett! Happy to help you!" Lina yelled, making sure to draw attention to the fact that Brett had talked with her.

SIXTEEN

The Chitchat Supper Club had been family-owned ever since it opened just after World War II. In the many following decades, the decor and food hadn't really changed, much to the delight of its customers, except there was less lake perch on the menu on account of overfishing. Supper clubs in Wisconsin weren't the same as "supper clubs" in big cities like New York, Los Angeles, or Amsterdam. In those places, a supper club usually meant some sort of burlesque joint, or an underground-hipster dining experience that used a quaint, ironic name in order to underscore its cool factor. Either way, a New York supper club would definitely disappoint the entire grandma population of America's Dairyland. Grandpas might be OK with it, as long as brandy were available with the T and A.

Supper clubs in Wisconsin were exactly as advertised, i.e., family-friendly restaurants in rural areas that opened for supper and served retro food and drink because "we've always done it this way." The name came from post-Prohibition Wisconsin, when liquor licenses were mainly issued to establishments that served food, most of them located in the countryside. The original supper clubs provided an entire evening's worth of entertainment to a crowd of farmers, bankers, shop owners, and their dates, so there was no need to go anywhere else.

The Chitchat's location had originally been a tavern that was built at the end of World War I. It was then purchased in the late 1940s by John Petersson a few months after he got married, and he and his wife turned it into a hangout for post-hunting-and-fishing dinner and dancing. Over time, it became Mistake's most popular supper club, especially after the Bluegill burned down because of a grease fire during a Friday fish fry. Following John's death, his son, Jim, took over the restaurant with his wife, Daphne, who acted as hostess, and his daughter Becky, with whom he tended bar.

The staple drink of supper clubs, besides beer, was the brandy old-fashioned served sweet or sour. Forget about a normal whiskey old-fashioned in Wisconsin—those were as unheard-of as not being able to buy brandy at the grocery store. Neither Becky nor her dad cared if an out-of-state guest ordered an old-fashioned with a specific whiskey, because they'd still make it with brandy, hand it to the guest, and proclaim, "This is Wisconsin." Brandy was as Northwoods as loons, bears, and muskies. It was in everything, from cocktails to Thanksgiving cranberry sauce to Christmas chocolates.

The Troll was on his second brandy old-fashioned sour and playing with a dating app on his phone when Tom "The Hammer" Hammerli sat down beside him at the bar. Much like the Troll, the Hammer's nickname easily derived from his last name. Unlike the Troll, the Hammer's nickname also described his strong-armed business tactics that the Troll probably didn't fully grasp.

"You're late," the Troll complained as he put his phone away in his pocket. He was annoyed that he had to buy two drinks while waiting.

"I know," the Hammer said nonchalantly. "But that shouldn't concern you as much as this task-force stupidity."

"I'm sure the sheriff will find them soon, and this will all be over." The Troll had no idea if this was true, but he didn't know what else to say.

"I don't give a crap about the mailboxes or when they find them."

"The mayor is really behind the MMTF—"

"Are you listening? I said I don't care."

"I can't stop them from looking—"

"Then what the hell am I paying you for?"

The Hammer had been paying the Troll for the past two years to keep the prying eyes of the government away from his business in Castor Forest. The Troll's payment of choice? A full annual membership at Lake Mistake Country Club. The Hammer thought that was weird as hell because everyone else that he'd ever bribed wanted cash, but it was all the same to him. It wasn't as if he'd ever be caught dead hanging out at that preppy golf course, anyway.

Castor Forest was originally named *Le Forêt des Castors*, or Beaver Forest, by French Canadian explorers who harvested the animals for the massive fur trade of the eighteen hundreds. The superb success of the fur trade meant that no beavers had been seen in the forest for a hundred years, felling trees for dams, so the woods grew denser. Most of Castor Forest was located in La Jolie County, with a small portion spilling into Waumabenon County. It was on this Waumabenon County section that the Hammer managed a successful marijuana farm. He had hired the Troll to keep away all government officials, such as overeager parks and recreation employees who might want to build something stupid like a walking path or playground.

The job wasn't too difficult for the Troll because he found that constantly spreading rumors about a venomous-snake infestation in the forest did the trick. He had been inspired after watching a program about the tree snakes in Guam. It was a genius move. Environmentalists instantly protected the snakes, sight unseen, from any development, and regular folks steered clear of the area because they didn't want their weekend picnic served with a side of venom.

But now the Musky Mailbox Task Force was poking around too close for comfort, albeit with animal control by its side. The ruse would soon be revealed, and the Troll would have to find another reason to keep people out of the forest. He had cooked up a scheme to plant a ton of poison-ivy seeds. Or poison oak. Whichever was more poisonous, as he always forgot. The Troll made a mental note to do an Internet search when he got home, then realized that the Hammer was snapping his fingers in his face.

"Hello! Are you listening to me? Get them away from my weed!" The Hammer reached over, stuck his fingers in the Troll's old-fashioned, and removed the brandy-soaked cherry. "Or you can say good-bye to your boathouse." He popped the cherry into his mouth and left.

The Troll simmered with anger over the threat and the poached cherry, which was his favorite part of an old-fashioned. On one hand, the Troll had the Hammer to thank for recommending his services as a fixer to Whole Lotta Bait for securing their store's building permit, which would lead to his boathouse permit. On the other hand, this made him very vulnerable to the Hammer. He'd heard rumors about people who defied the Hammer. Apparently those people ended up saying hello to Klaus Heffelfinger at the bottom of the cranberry bog.

The Troll waved to Becky Petersson with his empty glass. "I'll have another."

SEVENTEEN

Megan and Lina had been planning their mom's fortieth birthday ever since Mr. "You Can Call Me Pete" Helstrom's party several years ago. On the morning of the big day, a large lawn sign shaped like a bear appeared by the driveway and wished Pete a "Beary Good 40th Birthday." All the neighborhood kids thought it was really neat, and ever since that day Megan and Lina were determined to have one for their mom. Megan secretly wished her parents would get her one next year when she turned seventeen on June 17, her golden birthday.

The girls convinced their dad to buy a similar sign shaped like a cow that said, "Hay there, Cheryl! Have an udderly great 40th!" Cheryl got such a kick out of it when she saw it on the front lawn that she must have taken more than a dozen photos, about three of which weren't blurry.

The birthday celebration continued into the evening with a family trip to the Chitchat. The third relish tray was sitting on the lazy Susan when Cheryl's sister arrived. Sheriff Holm was finally off duty after a long day of Musky Mailbox Task Force interviews that uncovered a surprising number of old folks who believed in a super-strength chipmunk conspiracy. Even Ruth Tryggestad, widow of City Council Member Patrick Tryggestad, firmly believed that chipmunks had absconded with her musky mailbox.

"There's no chipmunks for months and months," she said when Sheriff Holm interviewed her. "All of a sudden, my yard is overrun with hundreds of chipmunks."

"Pretty sure they came out of hibernation this month. It was a long winter."

Ignoring the sheriff, Ruth continued. "Then suddenly, one morning, *poof*, my mailbox is gone."

"I think it's just a coincidence that they emerged from their burrows at the same time."

"They're up to no good. Never forget 1974, sheriff."

The Northwoods had always been prime real estate for Wisconsin weirdos, and this woman clearly was no exception. When Sheriff Holm walked into the Chitchat that night, she waved to Ruth, who was sitting at the bar.

"Never forget," Ruth said to the sheriff.

Oh, I won't, Sheriff Holm thought as she walked toward her family.

"She's finally here!" Todd said warmly. "We put in an order for the walleye special."

"I saved a seat for you, Aunt Lori!" Lina patted the open seat next her.

Gunnar Smith appeared next to Megan. "Are you finished with the relish tray? Do you want more soda? Do you need me to clear anything else?" Ever since he'd started clearing tables as a busboy two months ago, Gunnar always dedicated special attention to the Svensons because of his unrequited crush on Megan.

"We haven't even gotten dinner yet," Megan said, exasperated. "What's there to clear?"

"OK, just, you know, wave." Gunnar left, and Megan rolled her eyes.

"Gunnar and Megan sitting in a tree, k-i-s-s-i-n-g!" Lina never let a moment like this slide, but she secretly wished that Brett paid as much attention to her.

"Shut up!"

"Happy birthday, sis." Sheriff Holm hugged Cheryl. "Sorry I'm late. Got tied up." She sat in the seat next to Lina.

"Oh? Any news? Todd's been hearing all sorts of theories at the custard stand, haven't you, hon?"

"Oh, yeah, some of your guys said that they've been driving all over town asking questions."

"Do you think the thieves are as dangerous as Mayor Ole says?" Cheryl was always concerned about vandalism, even though the Svensons had never been vandalized. Melanie Chevalier's daily crime reports made Cheryl very, very nervous and, therefore, a very, very dedicated Lake News 37 viewer.

"No, just some kids being stupid, I'm thinking."

"Exactly, and it could be kids from Waunomonee or wherever," Megan jumped in. "But no, the Troll has to punish—"

"Let's not go through all of that again," Todd interrupted.

"But it's true!" She turned to her aunt. "Canceling Opening Day isn't going to catch anyone, will it?"

"Not really, no."

"See?"

Cheryl managed to steer the dinner conversation back to more important things, like whether the family's summer road trip would be to Wisconsin Dells or somewhere more exotic like Mackinac Island.

"We could go to the same place as Christopher Reeve and Jane Seymour," Cheryl said with a smile.

"Who are they?" Megan asked.

"Ugh. I don't want to hang out with your annoying friends from college," Lina moaned. The girls were unaware that their mom was referring to the filming location for the 1980 movie *Somewhere in Time*, a film that no one their age had ever heard of or seen because it was so last millennium.

After Gunnar cleared their dinner plates, the Svensons ordered dessert. The adults devoured a fancy birthday Baked Alaska (made special by Daphne Petersson) while the girls sipped on their very Wisconsin, very alcoholic milkshakes. Megan loved Brandy Alexanders, but Lina thought brandy was gross, so she ordered a grasshopper one instead.

The Baked Alaska was pretty messy, and as they were making fun of Todd's chocolate-covered face, an unwelcome drunk voice asked, "Sheriff, why aren't you out looking?"

"Deputy mayor." Sheriff Holm smiled through her gritted teeth. "So nice to see you."

"You should be detectiving for the mailboxes!" the Troll slurred, gesturing to the door.

"I was. All day. And now it's my sister's birthday."

"And don't detective in the forest. Especially in Castor Forest! Why would there be anything there? There aren't even beavers, and it's beaver forest!"

"OK, well, thanks for the tips."

"Detect somewhere else. You should detective in the high school!"

"Hey!" Megan yelled.

Gunnar instantly appeared out of chivalry, even though he didn't want to be associated with any conversation regarding mailboxes, especially in front of the sheriff. "Is the Troll bothering you, Megan?"

"You should be searching their lockers, their cars, their gym lockers, their—"

"You know, it's probably time for you to head home." Sheriff Holm got up and waved to the hostess stand. "Daphne, can you call the station? Have someone come take the Troll home?"

Daphne nodded and picked up the phone. It was her third call that night for someone to collect a friend after too many old-fashioneds. Usually, she'd made at least six calls by seven p.m.

"Hey, I don't want any coppers at my home!" the Troll said, waving his arm at imaginary deputies.

"They're just dropping you off."

"Dropping me off?"

"Dropping you off."

"Fine! They can come to the corner, but no farther."

"Okeydoke."

"Not in my house."

"Yeah, I got it."

"Not in my yard."

"Gunnar, can you walk him outside?"

Gunnar stepped toward the Troll, who recoiled but didn't resist. The Troll looked at him and said, "You know where the mailboxes are!"

Shit! Gunnar froze.

Then the Troll turned to Megan. "You know where they are!" And then Lina. And then any teenager he could see.

Whew, thought Gunnar. *He's just nuts.*

While pissed off to be in the WCSD car, the Troll went over his evening in his head as he slouched in the backseat. He was pretty sure that he'd smoothed things over with the Hammer and successfully redirected the sheriff's search efforts with his excellent powers of persuasion.

The Troll was dropped off at the end of his driveway despite strong protest to be left near the street corner. After the deputy drove away, he walked over to his pier to fantasize about his upcoming lifestyle improvement. Soon, the tarp-covered mound of steel and wood near his shed would be a beautiful boathouse.

It was at that moment that the Troll was struck with drunken inspiration to begin construction. Why not? Tomorrow was Wednesday! Permit day! He'd receive his precious boathouse permit! He looked at his phone for a message from Whole Lotta Bait. Nothing, but he wasn't worried about them keeping their word because Whole Lotta Bait was cool. The Hammer was cool. Everything was cool. Especially what he was about to start building. He picked up one of the steel piles and stumbled over to the lake. It was going to be so cool!

As the Troll was building away, Melanie Chevalier updated the Lake News 37 viewing area on the Musky Mailbox Mystery (roll the fancy graphics package!). "Tonight at ten: A power surge on Main Street zaps all traffic lights. How can you drive around Mistake and not die tonight? We have the tips to save your life. But first..." Melanie turned to one camera and lowered her voice. "Opening Day is canceled."

A new graphics package unrolled across the screen as a large red circle with a slash across it crashed onto a musky. "Deputy Mayor Kenny Trollqvist has canceled all Opening Day festivities until the Musky Mailbox Mystery is solved."

"This is astonishing news, folks!" Michael Gunderson interjected. "No fishing contests, no parties, no bait-the-hook contest, no day off from school!"

"According to the Troll, the main suspects are local teenagers, and the cancellation is a punishment until they come forward. Let's hope that Sheriff Holm and her Musky Mailbox Task Force crack this case soon."

"And on a lighter note, let's check in with Bob and Bonnie!" Michael said. "I hear she's got a new shirt today, Melanie!"

Tape rolled on the Bob-and-Bonnie piece. Their favorite lake hadn't thawed, so they were still in their boat in their driveway. Bonnie was indeed wearing a new T-shirt. Crafty moms loved Bonnie, especially the crafty moms who used the word *craft* as a verb, as in, "I like crafting and telling everyone about all of my crafting, so that I can feel better about myself for spending three hours on your birthday card that you didn't even know was handmade until you turned it over and saw my handmade stamp on the back." Bonnie never used *craft* as a verb. She was too busy fishing to worry about turning her kitchen's breakfast nook into a gift-wrapping station with two dozen types of ribbon mounted to the wall. She'd rather mount something on the wall like the new musky that she'd just painted on her T-shirt.

Her T-shirts were a fun tradition that she'd started before "Fishin' with Bob 'n' Bonnie." Viewers loved the homey touch of their beloved Bonnie painting a true-to-size fish of the largest catch of the past week on her shirt. The head would start on her left side, then curl around her stomach so that the tail would meet the head. That was the idea, even though it usually didn't happen because Bonnie was on the heavier, apple-shaped side. There were a couple of times when she'd caught such a long fish that the tail went past the head. Bonnie excitedly referred to these shirts as wraparounds.

"Muskies are finally biting, looks like!" Bonnie pointed to her shirt. "The water's crystal clear with the melting ice. And the temperature is still cold, so be sure to use your small crankbaits and bucktail spinners. Fish them slow, because monster muskies are ambushers, not chasers."

"Then make sure you do a good figure eight to land 'em when they strike," added Bob. "And don't forget to eat some Brinkerhoff Brats to give you the energy you need for a day of fishing!"

Bob and Bonnie grabbed two brats with sauerkraut and said together, "Brinkerhoff Brats. So much wurst, ya know it's the best." Then each of them took a big bite.

"Fishin' with Bob 'n' Bonnie" had been sponsored by Milwaukee's Brinkerhoff Brats for the past three years, a deal that had turned out to be incredibly successful and lucrative for both parties. The sponsorship kicked off with a bang when Bob nearly set fire to his boat after he'd overestimated the amount of lighter fluid one needed while trying to grill onboard in windy conditions. Bonnie pushed the flaming mini grill overboard with one of Bob's fishing poles—she certainly wasn't going to use one of her own—and Bob had screamed, "Not the Brinkerhoff! Aw, jeez! I'm starving, Bonnie!" It was the kind of viral-video publicity that Brinkerhoff Brats didn't know they could buy.

EIGHTEEN

Todd Svenson was obsessed with pinball machines. As a child, he spent so many hours playing them at Fun Times World arcade that his mom had convinced the owner (with a bottle of California's finest brandy) not to let her son inside the door during summer. Then Todd became an adult and realized that the best thing about being an adult was the ability to buy a whole pinball machine for himself. One led to two, two led to three, and so on until his entire basement became wall-to-wall filled with pinball machines.

This annoyed Cheryl for three reasons: 1) She couldn't easily get to the back of the basement, and oh, dear, what if it floods, and she can't see water damage, and there's hidden black mold, 2) She had to crawl under the pinball machines twice a week in the summer to wait out tornado warnings, and 3) She didn't have enough space to store her growing collection of Christmas and Halloween decorations. The only available storage space in the basement was under those darn pinball machines, which worried her because her treasures were on the floor and floods were inevitable, according to Melanie Chevalier and the Lake News 37 team.

Storage space was always a source of friction between Cheryl and Todd. Cheryl hated having to get on the floor and crawl seven feet under the pinball machines to get to the winter sweaters when the weather turned cold. Todd always thought this was a teachable moment about reducing the amount of clothes and junk that one owned. All of his clothes fit into just three drawers. Then Cheryl would remind Todd of The Dinner Party Incident, which would silence Todd on the storage issue until spring, when the cycle repeated itself.

Two years ago, Cheryl was hosting a dinner party for the crème de la crème of Mistake—Bob and Bonnie, plus Melanie Chevalier's hairdresser!—when Lake News 37 issued a tornado warning. Cheryl was mortified to usher her VIP guests into the basement, where they had to awkwardly crawl under the pinball machines to wait out the storm. To make matters worse, a mouse family with its extended relatives had just moved in under the oldest machine. Discovery of the mouse house caused the first ever pinball-related stampede, forcing nine adults to spend thirteen uncomfortable minutes crammed together under the stairs as if it were rush hour on the New York subway.

The mice had been eradicated, but mousetraps now littered the Svensons' dark basement floor like land mines. Stored somewhere under pinball machine number four, five rows deep and near the water softener, was a plastic bin that contained all of Cheryl's summer fishing gear. Thanks to her birthday hangover, she was in no mood to crawl around the booby-trapped basement that Wednesday morning, so she sent Megan downstairs to find her Opening Day clothes before her daughter went to school.

Megan also hated the pinball machines, but only because they prevented her family from being able to finish-off the basement and make it a place to hang with her friends. She switched on the basement light, counted the number of machines under which she needed to crawl, and got down on her knees with a flashlight. About five feet in, she suddenly saw multiple sets of glowing eyes and froze dead in her tracks. Her heart stopped for a second as her mind raced through the possibilities of the animals that could be lurking in the back of the basement, ready to attack like The Dinner Party Incident.

She quickly pointed the flashlight to the horrifying eyes and saw...two dozen musky mailboxes shoved under the pinball machines at the far reaches of the basement. In that moment, she knew exactly who had been stealing them.

While Megan thought about what to do, the crew for Lake News 37 was setting up on the edge of Waushauna Lake. Producers wanted to interview fishermen who were annoyed with the cancellation of the Opening Day fishing contest, and they hoped to find some really angry people who wanted to be on TV and didn't care how dumb they looked. The key to local news coverage was finding people with a complete lack of shame in order to fill five hours per day of local affiliate time with the cheapest programming available.

While unloading the news van, a cameraman noticed an unusually large hole in the melting ice far away from shore. He first thought it was just part of the thaw, but then he realized that ice didn't start melting with a huge jagged hole in the center of the lake. No one to his knowledge had been reported missing, but he got goose bumps at the possibility of a great story. He immediately called his producer with the news. The producer then called the WCSD and promised information in exchange for exclusive access to the story, if there were a story. She was a great local-news producer who always had her priorities in line. Her number-one priority was high ratings for a program that only older people watched, no matter how sexy, fun, and entertaining the news became in order to attract younger eyeballs.

NINETEEN

The morning teenage gossip fest ended when the first-period warning bell rang at 7:50 a.m. Brett closed his locker, turned around, and immediately saw Megan's judgmental face staring back at him.

"Get outta here, Svenson."

Megan thought back to when Brett's teasing abruptly stopped in ninth grade. Every once in a while, for the right amount of cash, she'd agreed to babysit his little brothers. Mrs. Brabender paid really well since it was difficult to get any neighborhood teen to agree to Toxic-Twin-and-Vince duty after the boys trapped Jennifer Frigaard, Bridget's older sister, in the bathroom so that they could continue constructing a flaming skateboard ramp in the kitchen without her annoying negativity.

During the one time last year that she'd babysat, Megan discovered a framed photo of Brett and platinum-selling French chanteuse Brigitte Claire Lamoureux, a favorite of grannies around the world, from Brett's thirteenth birthday trip to Las Vegas. He'd told everyone at school that he went to see wrestling, but he'd really gone to see his favorite middle-aged singer. Brett promised to stop the teasing forever if Megan never told anyone or put a copy of the photo online. Instantaneously, her life became much more pleasant.

Megan didn't anticipate that she'd once again be in a position to confront Brett with hubris-destroying photographic evidence, but she was in that position that morning, and she was loving every second of it.

"What do you want, Svenson?"

Megan silently raised her phone, and Brett came face-to-face with a picture of the musky mailboxes stashed under the pinball machines.

"Crap." He looked around for lurking teachers or Principal Jansen and lowered his voice. "Look, your sister said it was fine."

"Of course she'd say it's fine. She's been obsessed with you since sixth grade."

"Then we're cool?"

"No! Opening Day was canceled because of you!"

"Keep your voice down! It was canceled because the Troll is an asshole."

"Yes, but you encouraged his assholery." Megan shrugged her shoulders. "And this time he was right. Which kinda sucks."

"He's such a dirtbag."

"When are you getting them out of my house?"

"I don't know. Whenever your aunt stops snooping around everywhere."

"You better hope there are no storm warnings. You know my mom will find them during the first one that Melanie Chevalier tells her about."

"I know, I know. I'm working on it."

"I could end this now, you know. All I have to do is call my aunt, and we get Opening Day back like this." Megan snapped her fingers.

"Just give me more time."

"It's the day after tomorrow!"

"Please, don't tell anyone!"

"What's in it for me?"

Brett thought for a moment. "Mutually assured self-destruction. The mailboxes are all in *your* house."

"Oh, come on!"

"And it really helps the case against you guys that Lina loves posing for photos." Brett showed his phone to Megan, which displayed a picture of a smiling Lina organizing the mailboxes under the pinball machines.

"Ugh. Why does she lose her mind around you?"

"Brabender charm," Brett said with a smile. "So, what are we going to do?"

"We?"

"Yeah, remember they're in your—"

"Yeah, yeah." An idea began to percolate in Megan's head. "You're gonna need to borrow your dad's truck tonight. And I'm coming with. I don't want you screwing it up."

TWENTY

Mistakers were a kind bunch of folks. Always there to help their neighbors fend off a pack of angry wild turkeys, or let them know that their dog was running amok after squirrels on the other side of the neighborhood. But keeping an eye on tourists? Well, they were pretty easy to lose track of because they were similar-looking people doing similar things on a rotating basis.

So it really wasn't so much about their dislike for Chicagoans that no one noticed when three businessmen went fishing and never returned to their cabin. It was just more of a general laissez-faire attitude toward indistinguishable visitors. Besides, no one from Whole Lotta Bait thought to call Shady Pines Lodge to ask about their colleagues, even though it was odd that Leclerc, McCool, and Schweitzman had not responded to e-mails about an upcoming Cubs tailgate. The Whole Lotta Bait marketing team just figured that Schweitzman's party took an extremely fun and surprising turn straight out of every Hollywood movie about bachelor parties. *Schweitzman, man, always livin' the dream*, his boss thought.

Sheriff Holm arrived at Waushauna Lake just as the sunken SUV was being pulled from the water. The ice was melting so quickly in the rapidly warming weather that the recovery unit just smashed a path through the remaining ice to access the open hole with boats of divers. The team was on its way back to shore with three bodies, all middle-aged men that no one recognized. The last time they'd pulled a body from the lake was several months ago, when Mr. Fresvik dove into an ice-fishing hole in pursuit of the smartphone that he'd dropped while hammered on Christmas glogg.

Of course, Lake News 37 fervently recorded the recovery that morning, led by the tenacious producer who had secured the exclusive and the one cameraman trying to cover all angles. His favorite angle was always canted, low to the ground, where no one could really tell what was going on but it looked like an artsy film-school shot. That was the most important thing to local news cameramen.

Deputy Svingen waved to Sheriff Holm as she exited her car. "Hey! How was your sister's birthday?"

Sheriff Holm gestured for him to wait a second. She couldn't speak because her mouth was too full of chocolate frozen custard from the cone she was holding. It was after ten a.m., after all. She swallowed and answered, "Oh, good. It was the walleye special."

"Mr. Petersson sure does the best walleye."

"Oh, yeah," she agreed. She nodded in the direction of the lake. "So what's going on here?"

"Dive team is bringing in three bodies now. Plates on the car are Illinois."

"And they drove out on the ice last night?"

"Must have been a couple of days ago. The ice wouldn't have held a car to get that far out last night."

"No kidding."

"Hey, they still doing the walleye tonight?"

Squealing tires came to a halt behind the sheriff, and the Troll leaped from his car, looking completely disheveled. "Sheriff! Sheriff, I need to speak with you!"

For Pete's sake! "Look, Mr. Trollqvist, the deputy dropped you off at your driveway instead of the corner because it was really dark and—"

"What? No, I don't care about that." The Troll gestured to the chaotic scene on the lake. "Who died? The news said it was Chicagoans."

"The victims? All we know is that the plates are Illinois."

"OK." The Troll's brain processed away, trying to figure out a course of action in case his boathouse permit was lost at the bottom of the lake. His mind was fuzzy from the hangover that he was trying to hide. He'd woken up sprawled on his kitchen floor, holding a hammer. He didn't remember why he had the hammer, but it was an appropriate analogy to the current hammering in his head. "So they went into the water this morning, then?"

The sheriff stared at the Troll, trying to figure out why he cared about three possible Chicagoans' deaths. "You know, if you're here because of the mailboxes, no one found anything in their car."

"Mailboxes?"

"Yeah. The musky mailboxes."

"Right! Well, why would they be in their car? They're not teenagers."

"Why are you here?" *And why do you look like a guy who just emerged from five months in an ice-fishing shack?*

"It's a city tragedy! Tourists are dying! I may need to make a statement."

"Sheriff!" a diver yelled. The boat was docked, and the bodies were lying on the pier.

Sheriff Holm and Deputy Svingen walked over, the Troll close behind. The diver held up an assault rifle, its wet strap dangling, and pointed toward one of the bodies. "This fella had this on him."

"It's mine!" the Troll yelled as he pushed his way toward the bodies.

"The rifle?" Sheriff Holm asked.

The Troll finally saw what the diver was holding. *Crap.* "Oh, no. I, um, I meant to say, 'It's fine.' Yeah, it's fine. You guys have this under control, for sure. No statement needed. We can keep this"—he was going to say *quiet*, until he saw the Lake News 37 crew—"out of a task force. Not necessary. Speaking of which, I'd appreciate an e-mail update this evening, Sheriff."

"Not sure how much news we'll have by then. The autopsy won't even be finished."

"What? No, an update on the Musky Mailbox Task Force."

"Sheriff, I have their wallets." Deputy Svingen was holding three wet drivers licenses. "All Illinois. They're from Chicago."

Thinking back to her conversation with Krumpelmann at the Nimrod, Sheriff Holm asked, "Mr. Trollqvist, are you sure you don't know these men?" She turned back to the Troll, but he was already in his car and peeling out of the parking lot. He wanted to get to a safe place immediately to contact the Hammer and discuss the inconvenient deaths of the men who had his precious boathouse permit.

Sheriff Holm sighed and bit into her frozen-custard cone in frustration as she watched him disappear into the distance. While she chewed and thought about what the Troll knew about the three Chicago guys, she noticed that a blob of chocolate was on her uniform. "*Uff da!*" As the last body bag was being zipped up behind her, she wiped the frozen custard from her chest and groaned, "Well, that's gonna leave a stain."

TWENTY-ONE

Gunnar couldn't believe it. Megan was in his house. To see *him*, not his sister! Well, more like she was in his yard. And crouched in the bushes with him and Brett. But she was still only ten feet from his bedroom. He had been squished up next to her, smelling her hair, when she pushed him away and made Brett sit between them.

"You said he goes to bed at nine thirty!" Megan hissed, gesturing to the house.

"He normally does. Just wait a little longer," Gunnar said. "We can go wait in my room. You can see his house from my bed."

"In your dreams."

You are, Gunnar thought. *You are.*

Megan checked the time on her phone. "It's almost ten p.m. My mom is gonna kill me."

"Who cares?" Brett said.

"I know you don't."

"Obviously."

Megan glared at the illuminated house. "It's like he's doing this on purpose." She turned to Brett. "We're going straight home after this."

"Maybe I wanna get a custard."

"We are not stopping at my dad's store!"

"Too bad you don't have a license. Looks like you have to come with."

"Then I'm walking home."

"Five miles in the dark? You better watch out for the Skog."

"Grow up."

The Skog monster was a mythical beast that lived in the dense forests of the Wisconsin Northwoods. *Skog* meant "forest" in Swedish and Norwegian, but over time it became wholly associated with the name of the creature who stalked through the woods from dusk till dawn. Strange, unexplained occurrences in Mistake were sometimes blamed on the Skog monster, like a strong gust of wind that blew away all the napkins at a picnic, or all of the tomatoes being eaten overnight from someone's garden. Mostly, though, the Skog was a bogeyman that moms and dads used, such as, "You better get back from Lauren's house before dinner, or the Skog will get you," or "Don't go too far into the woods where the Skog lives. You don't want to make him mad." The Troll also liked the Skog for helping him keep curious little kids away from Castor Forest.

"Forget about walking. We're going to be together the whole night, Megan. Dusk till dawn."

"Ugh, kill me now."

"But then I'd have to clean up the mess. You know how I hate cleaning."

"Hey! Look!" Gunnar pointed. The house lights had just been switched off.

"Finally!" Megan stood up. "Come on." Gunnar and Brett followed Megan as she ran into the Troll's yard.

Gunnar only made it a few steps before falling flat on his face. He'd been staring at Megan's butt as she ran, and he'd failed to notice the newest addition to his mom's family of Swedish garden gnomes.

Next time, thought Gunnar, *we're stealing these stupid gnomes instead of mailboxes.*

"Gunnar!" Megan whispered angrily. "Stop screwing around!"

What a woman!

TWENTY-TWO

After escaping their annoying wives, Old Geezer One and Old Geezer Two were enjoying their eighth cigarettes of the day on the Nimrod Lodge porch and listening to the comforting American sounds of the Mistake Gun Club located down the road. But their peaceful morning was disturbed by Sheriff Holm, who strode up the steps and quickly walked inside without even acknowledging their existence.

"Whoa!" said Old Geezer One. "What's the rush, sweetheart?"

Old Geezer Two yelled through the screen door, "Watch out, guys! Wild dame on the loose!" Then he turned to his buddy and said, "Hope she's not on her monthly."

"Don't worry," said Old Geezer One. "She's not." He took a wheezy drag on his cigarette. "Two more weeks."

Old Geezer Two turned to his friend. "Two more weeks, eh?"

"Maybe less." Without missing a beat, Old Geezer One lit a new cigarette.

The sheriff found Wayne Krumpelmann at the bar and Grand Leader Eckerstorfer glaring at her as he cleaned his hunting rifle. Krumpelmann was on the phone, trying to convince someone at Mistake Lutheran to cancel the next lutefisk supper because it conflicted with the lodge's *Syttende Mai* dance.

"Yeah, I know everyone looks forward to lutefisk, but this is once a year, you know. And I think that everyone looks forward to the dance, too. I mean, can't you reschedule, like you do when the Pack are playing? Okeydoke, all right then. See you on Sunday, Pastor Jennifer."

Krumpelmann hung up and gave a thumbs-up to Eckerstorfer.

Sheriff Holm greeted the two, then handed Krumpelmann several photos of the three men pulled from the lake.

"Oh, yeah, that's them," Krumpelmann said. "They were the Chicago guys talking to the Troll out back."

"Did you hear anything they were discussing?"

"No, I was too far away. Plus, the lawn was getting mowed, so, you know, I couldn't hear anything."

Casey Eckerstorfer, handsome varsity quarterback of the Mistake High football team, entered the room, carrying a mayo jar. "Is this what you were looking for, Dad? It was still in recycling."

"Thanks," Grand Leader Eckerstorfer said as he took the jar from his son. He turned to Sheriff Holm. "Here."

"Wait, wait, wait!" Sheriff Holm cried. "I said don't touch it!" She held open a plastic evidence bag. "Just drop it right in."

Eckerstorfer paused a moment, annoyed that a woman was telling him what to do—and in his own lodge, for Pete's sake! He rolled his eyes and dropped the jar into the bag.

"Thanks," the sheriff said as she sealed the bag carefully so as not to disturb any remaining prints.

"We're very strict about picking up litter around the lodge," Eckerstorfer said. "That's why we still had it in recycling. Don't want anything to interfere with the loon habitats."

"What are you going to do with it?" asked Casey, who didn't know why anyone would want a smelly old jar.

"We'll see if there are any prints on it. See if maybe there's a connection between the Troll and these Chicago guys based off of what Mr. Krumpelmann told me about them," Sheriff Holm said.

"Did they share the mayo on a picnic?"

Sheriff Holm sighed. "Casey, shouldn't you be in school?"

"Nah, I took a long weekend," Casey said with the confidence that only a kid who was able to make his own rules thanks to a combination of movie-star looks, athletic ability, and Nimrod legacy could possess. "It's Opening Day."

"Maybe."

"Are we done here, Lori?" Eckerstorfer said. "I have a lodge to run, and your presence is interfering with the social activities."

"Oh, I'm sure that I'm not interfering with anything inside the lodge," Sheriff Holm said as she began walking away. Just before she stepped out onto the porch, she took a hard left and stopped at the cigarette vending machine near the coatroom. The machines had been illegal in Wisconsin for several years, but the previous sheriff had let the lodge keep theirs as a nod to Mistake's gangster history, when no one in government could tell them what to do. Sheriff Holm reached into her pocket, took out a bunch of quarters, and jammed the machine.

TWENTY-THREE

The Hammer had ignored thirteen calls from the Troll by the time he broke into Lil' Moose at Shady Pines Lodge. He didn't want any distractions while in the cabin, either, so he left his vibrating phone in his car that was parked around the back. He was looking forward to finally severing ties with that idiot in City Hall.

He had been having a leisurely morning, drawing up plans for cutting down fifty maple trees for his pot farm's expansion, when he was interrupted by his police scanner crackling to life. Most transmissions on the scanner were related to traffic accidents, tavern fights, or homes being toilet-papered. This morning, however, a few words caught his attention: *bodies*, *lake*, and *Illinois*. He turned up the volume and heard Deputy Svingen read the victims' names from their licenses back to dispatch.

"Morons," the Hammer mumbled.

He called the Kaczmarski cousins to let them know that their reconnaissance team had been wiped out in an apparent bachelor-party accident on the ice. Scottie was the most upset because the marketing dudes were stand-up bros who would do anything for the company, like the time that Leclerc did a bunch of keg stands for charity donations. Don, on the other hand, was wholly concerned with the possibility of police finding sensitive documents pertaining to Whole Lotta Bait in Lil' Moose, as well as any connection to the Troll. The Hammer told him not to worry and that he would head over to Shady Pines Lodge immediately.

It took the Hammer exactly seven seconds to break into the cabin. He thought back to the good old days of thirty years ago when it would have been five seconds quicker because of no locks on the doors. The owners first installed locks on the cabins after a bunch of suitcases were stolen while the occupants spent their evening drinking at the Nimrod. Said occupants failed to inform the owners and the WCSD that they were pretty sure the Hammer was responsible, because no one else would have targeted inconspicuous gym bags unless they knew that they were full of cash. Cash stolen from the Hammer.

Lil' Moose was a complete mess. Even with the luxury of daily maid service, the cabin looked like it hadn't been cleaned since the Clinton Administration. It wasn't that surprising, considering that it had been occupied by three men in their late thirties and early forties who regularly acted like they lived in a frat house. McCool even kept a photo of John Belushi as Bluto in his wallet, a find that puzzled Deputy Svingen. As the Hammer searched the cabin, he was mildly amused by the overconfidence of the three sub-par-to-average-looking men in their ability to get laid in northern Wisconsin after discovering a toiletry bag entirely filled with condoms.

The Whole Lotta Bait laptops and phones were easy to locate because they were all charging on the power strip next to the television, but the paperwork that he knew existed was harder to find. He spent a frustrating twenty minutes digging through luggage, fishing gear, and bags of venison jerky without finding the building permit that the Troll had tossed to the guys in the mayo jar. Exasperated and thirsty, he opened the fridge to grab a beer and came face-to-face with the bait-shop building permit sealed in a plastic bag. There was another piece of paper in the bag, which the Hammer realized was the permit that had been obtained from the corrupt Wisconsin state representative for the Troll's boathouse. The fridge apparently held the three most valuable things to the Whole Lotta Bait marketing team: beer, building permits, and pizza.

The Hammer placed Whole Lotta Bait's building permit inside his jacket pocket. He then cracked open a cold one, took a drink, and thought about how pleased he was with himself. Then he took out his lighter and ignited the Troll's boathouse permit out of spite. Whole Lotta Bait couldn't be connected to the Wisconsin state representative any more than any other company that utilized his particular brand of pay-as-you-go politics. The Hammer might have been inclined to hand over the boathouse permit had the Troll not been such an annoying, desperate little man. With a satisfied smile, he tossed the burning permit into the dirty fireplace, grabbed the bag of condoms, and left.

Meanwhile, the Troll was panicking about not being able to get in touch with the Hammer. He didn't know what to do. Was his permit at the bottom of Waushauna Lake, or was it in the pocket of a dead man, or was it somewhere in their cabin? After an hour of eating his feelings, the Troll decided to go to Shady Pines Lodge to look for himself.

It took him five minutes to break into Lil' Moose after a brief, scary moment when he thought that he'd lost his credit card between the door and door frame. When he grabbed the door handle to shake the card loose, he realized that it wasn't locked. He quickly stepped inside and caught his breath as he peeked out the window to see whether anyone had seen him. Satisfied that he had been a veritable James Bond in his breaking and entering, he began to rifle through the room. He was tempted to steal some of the trendy fishing gear, but he knew he'd be too nervous to use it. It might be special Whole Lotta Bait prototypes that cops could spot a mile away, so he left that stuff alone. He did steal two condoms that he found on the floor, though. He'd need them once his boathouse parties raged.

After thirty minutes, he gave up on finding his boathouse permit. Surely Whole Lotta Bait could get him a new one. He also didn't find the bait-shop building permit that he had tossed to the guys in the mayo jar a few days ago. *Must have sent it down to Chicago*, he thought.

He wasn't worried about that permit being traced back to him, even though he had forged it. If anyone on Mistake City Council demanded to see it once Whole Lotta Bait began construction, the Troll was certain that he had thought of every contingency. A lot of credit was due to City Council Member Patrick Tryggestad for having the foresight to die a few weeks ago. The Troll thought he was brilliant for forging the dead man's signature on the permit and backdating it to one week before Tryggestad had died of a heart attack at The Tip-Up, a greasy diner next to the Lake Stockholm boat launch. The Troll had even filed the matching fake papers at the city council archives in case reporters were nosy enough to look for proof that it was a real permit. They probably wouldn't. Since Mistakers were too nice for their own good, they weren't going to speak badly about a dead man who couldn't defend himself. A valid permit was a valid permit, even if it was a questionable permit signed by someone who had passed away. The construction would go ahead unchallenged.

With nowhere else to look in the cabin, the Troll grabbed a six-pack from the fridge and returned to his car. He tried calling the Hammer again. The call was finally answered, but the robotic voice on the other end told the Troll that the number was no longer in service.

TWENTY-FOUR

The phone rang in Sheriff Holm's empty office at the WCSD headquarters. The ringing stopped for a brief minute, then began again in earnest. An excellent assistant would have answered it the first time, knowing that Sheriff Holm wasn't in the office. An average assistant, sensing something urgent due to the persistent ringing, would have answered the second time around. A curmudgeonly assistant, like Mike Zwicky, wouldn't answer at all.

Not answer is exactly what Mike did that morning, which really annoyed Megan. She hung up on her third attempt to reach her aunt's office line and looked up the main number to the WCSD headquarters on her phone. Even though she had her aunt's cell number, she knew that she couldn't call it because no anonymous tipster would have it.

The phone rang twice before a receptionist cheerfully answered. "Good morning! Waumabenon County Sheriff's Department, Jessica Kuutti speaking. How can I help you today?"

Megan took a deep breath. She was calling from one of the only remaining pay phones in Mistake, on the corner of

Main Street and Helbacka Road, in front of the high school. In an effort to disguise her voice, she had a towel over the receiver, and she tried to sound as adult as possible so that she would be taken seriously.

"Yes, hello. I'd like to make an anonymous tip. An anonymous crime tip."

"Sure, what's this regarding?"

"You know, I've just been seeing some suspicious activity in the neighborhood."

"Whereabouts?"

"Well, it's a bit of a sensitive matter."

"That's OK. We won't take any of your personal information."

"Well, you see, it's the deputy mayor. There were some suspicious things happening last night at the Troll's house."

"And what would that be?"

"You know, he was just moving around a bunch of large stuff in the dead of night. Real strange-like. All the same shape. There was a huge pile of them. Maybe two dozen, all under a tarp. I just noticed it earlier in the week. The covered pile, that is. But he was making a lot of noise. That's why I woke up and looked out my window."

"What do you think it is?"

"Jeez, I don't know. I mean, they were big, but he could carry them. He was doing it really late, so it seemed kinda suspicious." Megan took a long pause and said, "It sounds crazy, but it might be..." She paused again before whispering, "The mailboxes."

"Holy smokes! Thanks a lot for your call. We sure do appreciate it. Someone will be over to check it out as soon as possible."

"Thanks!"

"You betcha."

Megan hung up the pay phone and texted Brett: *Took care of it.* Then she ran back into school to get to chemistry.

Meanwhile, at the WCSD, Jessica Kuutti quickly dialed Sheriff Holm's cell phone to let her know about the hot tip for the Musky Mailbox Task Force.

TWENTY-FIVE

When the police SUV arrived in front of the Troll's house, he assumed they were finally coming to reprimand his neighbors, the Osthuses, for using the warming weather as an excuse to turn their front yard into extended basement storage space. The entire Pinewood neighborhood was tired of staring at plastic Christmas decorations, toboggan sleds, and all-weather plastic bins filled with old science fair projects.

An hour later, he wondered how everything could have fallen so spectacularly to pieces.

Sheriff Holm had knocked on his door and asked him about a late-night noise complaint that had been made against him. What the Troll didn't know was that while the sheriff was busy talking to him in the front of the house, Deputy Svingen was in a boat and eyeing his backyard from the lake side of his property. The WCSD had no search warrant, so Svingen was looking for any visible evidence of the mailboxes from the public lake while the Troll was distracted by the sheriff.

However, upon nearing the shore, it became immediately apparent to Deputy Svingen that the Troll was in the process of committing a much more serious crime—constructing an illegal boathouse. He was violating state law, which Deputy Svingen knew trumped county law for property theft.

He radioed to Sheriff Holm. "Sheriff? Deputy Svingen here. You're gonna want to come around back."

The Troll's eyes bulged from his face as he yelled, "Who's back there? You don't have any right to be here."

"Now, Mr. Trollqvist, there are just some deputies in a boat. On a public lake." Sheriff Holm picked up her radio. "Sheriff Holm here. You seeing a lot of muskies today?"

"Um, negative on the muskies so far, sheriff. But definitely seeing a state violation with this new boathouse."

The Troll denied that he had any knowledge of how five steel piles became haphazardly strewn about in the shallow water near his pier. Luckily for the Troll, they hadn't been driven into the bottom of the lake, despite his laughable nocturnal attempts to do so with a hammer instead of a pile driver. He insisted that since the piles were just sitting in the water, it didn't mean anything.

"Prove they're for a boathouse!" he challenged multiple times.

Unfortunately, he had spray-painted a message on his pier that read, "Welcome to the Troll's Boathouse." The message also included an arrow. The Troll certainly didn't want his invited guests to miss out on his parties.

The Troll frantically waved his arms around. "This is all a misunderstanding. And clearly vandalism! You should be out trying to find the teenagers who spray-painted my pier and threw the piles into the lake."

Sheriff Holm looked at the partially covered mound of remaining piles next to the large shed. "What are those for, then?"

"What's the difference to you? Maybe I'm building a deck. Maybe I'm building a pier. Maybe it's none of your business!"

"Do you have a building permit for a deck or a pier?"

The Troll gritted his teeth. "Not yet. But I don't need a permit just to own them."

"And this is your shed?" The sheriff stepped toward the shed and noticed another spray-painted message: "X. Boathouse here!"

She looked back at the Troll, who yelled, "Even more vandalism!"

At this point, the Troll had had enough. He just wanted them off of his property so he could call the Hammer and see what he should do. "I'm an American, you know. You can't just come onto my property."

He followed Sheriff Holm to the front of the shed. The door was ajar, and the sheriff peered into the dark space.

"Look!" the Troll exclaimed. "They unlatched the hook! I bet that's where the vandals stole my paint! You should dust for prints!"

The Troll swung open the door and found himself face-to-face with several dozen gleaming musky eyeballs from twenty-three musky mailboxes.

"Really?" the sheriff groaned.

"These aren't mine!" the Troll cried.

"Are you kidding me?"

"I've never seen these before! I swear!"

As the Troll's mind raced through the possibilities of how his shed became full of stolen property, he was interrupted by a bloodcurdling scream from the other side of the shed.

"Sheriff! Sheriff!" Deputy Svingen shrieked from the shoreline.

Sheriff Holm ran to the other side of the shed near the shore and looked at Deputy Svingen, who was nearly in tears.

"Sheriff, look!" The deputy pointed to a destroyed loon nest that had been crushed by a steel pile. If there was one thing Mistakers hated more than the missing musky mailboxes and Chicagoans, it was destroying a loon habitat.

"You monster!" he screamed at the Troll. "You monster! How could you?"

The Troll didn't remember much about what happened after Deputy Svingen punched him while screaming about loons being protected under the federal Migratory Bird Treaty Act of 1918. All he remembered was ending up with a black eye, wearing handcuffs, and sitting in the back of the sheriff's SUV, listening to her favorite country song for the entire drive back to WCSD headquarters.

It wasn't really Sheriff Holm's favorite Ben Kvam song, but as soon as "Sittin' in Handcuffs" came on, she punched the repeat button so she could watch the Troll squirm in her rearview mirror. She couldn't wait to call Megan with the good news.

TWENTY-SIX

The final bell rang late Thursday afternoon, and an elated student body ran out of school for a long weekend of Opening Day festivities. The great day of fishing the almighty musky had been restored immediately after the stunning arrest of the Troll earlier in the day for his crimes. The headline on *Uff Da* screamed, "Finally!" Principal Jansen had clocked out early during sixth period to fix her trolling motor, check her supply of heavy-braided spectra fishing line, and load her boat with beer. She was convinced that this would be the year that she'd join the fifty-inch club.

Megan was collecting homework from her locker when Brett walked over. "Nice work, Svenson."

"I told you the Troll was the perfect scapegoat."

"He's even more of a d-bag than I thought."

"Can you believe that he smashed a loon nest? I knew he was mean, but man."

"Uh-huh." Brett paused, awkwardly shifting his weight. "Hey, so I'm leaving now. Want a ride home?"

"A ride home? What, are we friends again?"

"You wish."

"What is it? Like, we teamed up to bring down the Troll, so an enemy of my enemy is my friend?"

"What?"

"Never mind." Megan closed her locker. "Let's go. We can get some new lures for tomorrow at your dad's."

That night Lake News 37 received its highest ratings since the Great Mistake Blizzard Weekend of 2009 when they debuted SnowPlowCam.

"Breaking news," Melanie Chevalier said. "The Musky Mailbox Mystery is closed." The Troll's mug shot popped up over her shoulder. "Deputy Mayor Kenny 'the Troll' Trollqvist has been arrested for stealing the musky mailboxes. Twenty-three of twenty-four mailboxes were discovered on his property today by Sheriff Holm. No word on the location of the twenty-fourth mailbox."

A video of Mrs. Helstrom immediately came up on screen. She was holding a photo of Mr. Postie and sobbing, "If anyone has seen him, please call me!"

Then, over b-roll of the crime scene in the Troll's backyard, Melanie described the stunning scene and chain of events. "In addition to terrorizing the city with the heinous crimes of musky-mailbox thievery, Deputy Mayor Trollqvist was also in the process of building an illegal boathouse, the construction of which destroyed a loon habitat. No word on the whereabouts of the devastated loon residents."

The video then cut to Sheriff Holm's statement at WCSD's headquarters. "We believe his motive for stealing the mailboxes was to create a distraction to cover up the boathouse. In regards to his vulgar ransom notes to Mrs. Helstrom, we believe his aim was to create maximum worry among the population with a very, very vocal target that would distract from the real crime."

Mayor Ole followed with his own statement that completely ignored the fact that his own deputy mayor had been arrested. "I'd like to say what a success my Musky Mailbox Task Force was! Thank you all for your help, my fellow Mistakers! We got our muskies back, everybody!" Mayor Ole then gave a thumbs-up to the camera, an image that the producers chose as the perfect freeze frame on which to stamp the graphics "Case Closed" across the screen before returning to the news anchors.

"Un-be-lievable, Melanie," Michael Gunderson said. "Un-be-lievable!"

"However, the one bright spot at the end of this tunnel of sadness?" Melanie asked.

"Opening Day is back!" Michael screamed at a level so loud that he even surprised himself. "That's right, folks! All Opening Day festivities are back on for tomorrow! So set your alarms and head on down to Lake Mistake to register for the Mistake Musky Classic fishing tournament that begins at six a.m. Kringle and coffee will be provided by Tomahawk Coffee. How about that?"

"And remember that all fishing-verification slips must be turned in by five thirty p.m. in order to be eligible for prizes, which will be presented by the one and only Bob and Bonnie," added Melanie, suddenly pressing her finger to her earpiece in order to imply that she was receiving very important information. "And I'm just being told that the world-famous Jake Anderssen's Water Ski Spectacular will be putting on a show tomorrow at noon!"

"The Waumabenonettes?"

"Yes, Michael."

"Oh, boy, folks, it's gonna be an unforgettable day! The Waumabenonettes!"

TWENTY-SEVEN

Upon being contacted by the WCSD and subsequently Lake News 37, Whole Lotta Bait disavowed all knowledge of the Troll's story that he had a valid permit to build his boathouse courtesy of the Chicago company. The Whole Lotta Bait public relations team described any notion that they had secured or were in possession of a special boathouse permit for the Troll as ludicrous, preposterous, slanderous, libelous, and "we have a lawyer on retainer."

According to the PR team, even if stories about the Troll talking to the Whole Lotta Bait team in the marsh were true, he was also illegally duck hunting, according to the witness. As for the prints on the mayo jar that connected the men? The Whole Lotta Bait team would obviously pick up any trash thrown at them by the Troll, because they were great guys who always recycled.

Fortunately for Whole Lotta Bait, all communication to the Troll had been funneled through the Hammer, so there were no records for the police to trace. The Troll had also been incredibly helpful to the cover-up effort by inadvertently dropping his Hammer-supplied burner phone into the lake when Sheriff Holm handcuffed him.

Whole Lotta Bait gained invaluable public sympathy by being in mourning for its dearly beloved colleagues who tragically died in Mistake. Mistakers actually felt sorry for these three Chicago guys after hearing the press release (read verbatim on Lake News 37 to fill airtime), extolling the Whole Lotta Bait team members "who died doing what they loved best: drinking, fishing, and shooting guns in the Wisconsin Northwoods."

Opening Day went ahead on Friday with great success. A record number of 1,083 registered musky anglers competed in the Mistake Musky Classic, sponsored by Brabender's Bait. Principal Jansen finally won the individual tournament by landing a fifty-one-inch musky with her lucky bucktail lure, placing fifteen spots ahead of her annoyed husband, John. Gunnar, the youth champion, even caught a bigger musky than John, cementing the principal's theory that John was the deadweight in the husband-and-wife team competition.

Lina also had a terrific Opening Day. Much like a golf caddy, she got to follow Brett around because she volunteered to carry his tackle box and net. It was pretty much the stuff of her dreams, except that he didn't allow her in his boat with his buddies. She also won a raffle for a fifty-dollar gift card to Nielsen's, which she planned on spending on a new swimsuit for summer tubing on the lakes in front of Brett.

Even though Megan spent most of Opening Day working the Svenson's stand near the polka band, she enjoyed discussing the Troll's downfall with everyone she met while scooping custard, including Brett, to whom she gave a free double scoop of Blue Moon. She had never felt more fulfilled at the justice finally served to the Troll, or, as she joked to the frozen custard customers, "Justice is best served cold with a wafer cookie." She was also happy to receive congratulations on becoming co-editor-in-chief of the school paper after her relentless investigative reporting helped end the Troll's reign of terror.

Brett had a winning day fishing and finished in the top five, which was pretty cool because it was seven spots higher than last year. It was also kinda-sorta cool that Megan was the winner of the seventeen-and-under Fastest Bait-the-Hook Contest. When he went over to congratulate her, he ended up surprising himself by giving her a hug. He ended up surprising himself even more when he kinda-sorta accidentally kissed her on the cheek.

"Ugh, what are you doing?" Megan protested as she pushed him away.

"I just thought...I mean, I...what are *you* doing?" stammered Brett. "You hugged me!"

"No, I didn't!"

"Yes, you did! Oh, boy, this is just like that *Single Sergio* episode!"

"What?"

"You know, the one where Kelly pretended that she had a crush on Sergio and then—"

"You're the worst!" Megan yelled. She ran away in search of a bathroom because she didn't know what else to do.

Witnessing all of this was a furious Lina. She couldn't believe her eyes! Megan knew that Brett was her boyfriend! Even if Brett didn't know, but that was a small detail. Lina started running after Megan when she saw Gunnar scaling a fish by the pier. If Megan kissed her boyfriend, then she was going to kiss Megan's.

"Hi, Gunnar!"

"Oh, hey, Lina! How about that—" Gunnar began until Lina shut him up by kissing him. "Whoa."

Lina looked around and realized that neither Brett nor Megan had seen her kiss Gunnar. "Ugh, where did they go?" She pushed Gunnar away and headed toward her friends in search of sympathy.

"What a woman!" Gunnar gushed as he watched Lina run away.

Later that Friday evening, when Mrs. Helstrom was letting her dog out before bed, she noticed something large on her front porch. She peeked through the blinds and recognized her beloved Mr. Postie. The WCSD hadn't been able to locate it in the Troll's shed, and she had been depressed all day. But now he had returned!

"He's back! Mr. Postie is back!" Mrs. Helstrom yelled to any family member who cared to listen—which was no one.

She opened the door and ran out to her porch. Curiously, Mr. Postie's flag was up. Mrs. Helstrom opened his mouth and saw a letter inside. Thinking it was a note from the WCSD, she quickly opened it. She immediately realized that she was reading more lurid tales of the sexual adventures that her mailbox had experienced since going missing, including photographs far worse than the Chicago Bears one.

"Oh, my stars," she mumbled, along with plenty of "no, no!" There was snickering behind her. She turned around to find her daughter, Taylor, reading over her shoulder. "Get to bed!" she yelled, and Taylor ran upstairs to post the video that she had recorded of her mom's reaction to Mr. Postie's return.

TWENTY-EIGHT

In the weeks that followed after the musky mailboxes were safely returned to their owners, multiple bombshells exploded all over Lake News 37, *Uff Da* by Megan Svenson, and the mom-gossip network. All were the result of Sheriff Holm holding what she considered the first legitimate press conference ever at City Hall. Megan was excited to attend her second press conference of the year.

"In light of new evidence based upon my investigation," she began, "I want to announce that all mailbox charges have been dropped against the Troll."

"What?" Megan screamed. "Aunt Lori! That's insane! He's guilty!" Not wanting to completely lie to her aunt, she quickly added, "He's totally guilty of the boathouse and the loons! And he'll just continue with his reign of terror!"

"He also resigned his position as deputy mayor this morning."

"Really? So he's no longer in charge of anything?"

"Nope."

"OK. No further questions." Megan smiled and sat down. It was the proudest moment of her life.

After the initial furor died down in the conference room, Sheriff Holm went on to explain that the Troll had been out of town for the first two nights of mailbox thefts. He had been in Mistake when the third group from Loon Hollow was stolen, but since he had a rock-solid alibi for the other nights—attending a Ben Kvam concert in Ottawaumegon with his mom—there was reasonable doubt as to whether he was involved at all. Besides, all mailboxes had been returned undamaged to their owners, so the city was fine with not pursuing any charges that would take up time during summer fishing season.

As for the other charges against the Troll, including the illegal boathouse and destruction of a loon habitat, they had been dropped due to a plea bargain. Luckily for the Troll, on the night that he'd met the Hammer at the Chitchat, he'd accidentally turned on the voice-memo function while playing with the dating app on his personal phone. These memos told Sheriff Holm about the Hammer's business in Castor Forest. The Troll immediately agreed to testify against the Hammer.

"As of this morning, the Tom 'the Hammer' Hammerli is in custody after being apprehended at his illegal marijuana farm."

Of course, all of this actual important news was quickly overshadowed by another discovery on the Troll's phone— incriminating photographic evidence of an affair between Principal Jansen's husband and Mrs. Helstrom. While taking photos of the Jansens' boathouse for construction ideas, the

Troll had inadvertently captured images of John Jansen and Mrs. Helstrom having sex in the boathouse during one of their regular rendezvous during school hours. Once the affair hit the gossip circuit, no one really cared about finding out who the real mailbox thieves were, anyway.

Later that year, Whole Lotta Bait and the Mistake Chamber of Commerce sent out a joint press release announcing the grand opening of the first Whole Lotta Bait, just in time for the annual fall Cranberry Festival that marked the anniversary of Klaus Heffelfinger being gobbled up by the bog. The official story from Whole Lotta Bait was that they wanted to open a memorial store in honor of their three colleagues who loved fishing in Mistake, and they just happened to own a plot of vacant land in the center of the city next to the Musky Slide. They also donated money—why the heck not?—to refurbish the slide so that it could reopen as soon as possible.

Even though Whole Lotta Bait had the forged building permit from the Troll, there was so much goodwill in the city after their PR assault in May that the company actually went through the official public process of getting a permit from the city council. The Kaczmarskis also felt a little sorry for the Troll for not getting his boathouse, even though he did them a major solid, so they made sure that he won a grand-opening contest for a pontoon party boat. The Troll didn't remember entering, but he certainly wasn't going to say anything.

Whole Lotta Bait also built a short twenty-foot Crappie Slide next to the Musky Slide for the kids that were too afraid to go fifty yards inside the musky tunnel. *Those Whole Lotta Bait guys are all right*, most Mistakers thought. The men in particular appreciated what Whole Lotta Bait brought to the bait-shop market in Mistake, i.e., Whole Lotta Girls. Business at Brabender's suffered the first few weeks until Bart realized that it would bounce back if he targeted families, which is how the weekly boob-free Brabender's Family Fun Daze began.

In honor of Sheriff Holm solving the most important crime of the century, Mayor Ole named her an honorary chair of the Cranberry Festival. Being an honorary chair basically meant that Sheriff Holm could skip straight to the front of every line, something that Mayor Ole did, regardless of honorary-chair status. But even better than being able to skip the line for brandy cranberry pie was getting engaged to her boyfriend by the picturesque bog in Heffelfinger Memorial Forest. It was the perfect proposal, with a diamond ring atop a Svenson's hot-fudge sundae.

A week later, Brett summoned the courage to ask Megan to the homecoming dance. He took a bag of colorful fake worms from the garage and spelled out "Homecoming?" on the step by her front door. The raccoons weren't the least bit interested in eating the message this time, so Megan actually saw it. She didn't know who it was from until she saw a small note in chalk that read, "From Brett, ran outta worms."

Against her better judgment, but in favor of the butterflies in her stomach, she said yes. When they went to the dance the next weekend, Megan wore her favorite scent, pumpkin pie. As a joke, she asked the DJ to dedicate three Brigitte Claire Lamoureux songs to Brett. He didn't mind at all.

MISTAKE MERCHANDISE

Stock up on Mattie the Musky gear to wear on Opening Day! Visit the *Mistake, Wisconsin* online store for official merchandise from Mistake High School, the Chitchat Supper Club, Brabender's Bait, and more.

www.cafepress.com/mistakewisconsin

GO MUSKIES!
MISTAKE HIGH SCHOOL ATHLETIC DEPT.
MISTAKE, WISCONSIN

ACKNOWLEDGMENTS

A big thank you to my friends and family for reading drafts of this Northwoods tale. I couldn't have written this without your support! Thank you to Sarah Williams and Liz Thottakara.

Thank you to my parents, Doug and Jayne, especially for your knowledge of all things Wisconsin. And thanks for the photo, Mom!

Erin Martin—I don't know how you found the time, but thank you for your invaluable advice and notes. A young adult book? You're the best, Erin!

And thank you to *you* for buying and reading my first book. I hope you had fun spending time in Mistake.

ABOUT THE AUTHOR

Kersti Niebruegge grew up in Wisconsin and caught her first fish (a walleye) when she was five. She graduated from the University of Wisconsin-Madison with a degree in journalism, and has worked for BBC Worldwide, *Conan*, and *Late Night with Seth Meyers*.

www.kerstiniebruegge.com
@kniebruegge on Instagram and Twitter

Made in the USA
Charleston, SC
19 December 2015